THE SECRET
SPANISH
LO...

CATHY WILLIAMS

MILLS & BOON

First published in Great Britain 2010
Harlequin Mills & Boon Limited,
Eton House, 18-24 Paradise Road, Richmond, Surrey TW9 1SR

© Cathy Williams 2010

ISBN: 978 0 263 87827 1

Harlequin Mills & Boon policy is to use papers that are natural,
renewable and recyclable products and made from wood grown in
sustainable forests. The logging and manufacturing process conform
to the legal environmental regulations of the country of origin.

Printed and bound in Spain
by Litografia Rosés, S.A., Barcelona

THE SECRET
SPANISH
LOVE-CHILD

CHAPTER ONE

GABRIEL heard his secretary's sharp rap on his office door with a sense of relief.

Perched on his desk, with her high, *high* heels dangling from her feet and her short, *short* skirt provocatively and purposefully riding high enough to expose a generous eyeful of thigh, Cristobel had been in full flow for the past twenty minutes.

She needed to *really start doing the shops*, the wedding was getting closer by the day and *everything had to be perfect* and there was just no way that she was going to leave *all the details* to that *ridiculous wedding planner* his mother had insisted on hiring.

She had punctuated each statement with a flick of her long, curling blonde hair and a jabbing motion with her finger, taking care to lean forward so that he couldn't fail to notice her deep cleavage and the full swell of her breasts under the tightly pulled silk top.

Cristobel was nothing if not sweepingly confident about her ability to use her body to its maximum advantage and while Gabriel would concede that he had been distracted by it for all of two minutes, right now he just wanted her out of his office and safely tucked away in whatever mind-blowingly expensive shop she favoured. He really didn't care. He had calls to make and several reports to look at and the high pitched, insistent staccato of her voice was beginning to give him a headache.

Naturally he had contained his impatience because she was, after all, his fiancée but he had almost given his secretary a standing ovation when she had tactfully suggested that she had checked the personnel files and found a Spanish speaking employee who would be delighted to take Cristobel to Knightsbridge, where she would be able to shop to her heart's content before she headed back to Madrid.

'But I want *you* to come with me,' Cristobel pouted now, leaning further forward and sweeping aside several documents as she planted her hands flat on his desk. 'It's important for you to get involved with the planning.'

'You don't want me involved with the planning, Cristobel,' Gabriel told her dryly. 'At any rate, you know how I feel about these things. Lavish weddings are not my cup of tea.' Nor, he mused now, were weddings of any sort, at least in so far as they pertained to him, until a year ago when he had finally and philosophically ceded to loving but insistent parental pressure.

His parents were both keen to see him married and settled. They were getting older. They wanted grandchildren. Whilst they were still at an age to enjoy them. Before they died.

And Gabriel had finally acknowledged that perhaps the time was right to take a wife. There was a very thin line between the desirable bachelor and the oldest swinger in town. He was now in his thirties and life had a habit of racing on.

Cristobel would make a perfectly suitable wife. Her family tree was as old as his was and as wealthy. She understood the unspoken rules of the way his life operated and would abide by them. Whatever she wanted, she would have and in return she would understand that his work was a priority for him. She was also a beautiful woman, small, voluptuous and well groomed.

On paper, it was a union brokered in heaven and any doubts were expertly fielded by using common sense and reason, two things which had never let him down in his life before.

'You'll enjoy Harrods with another woman.' His phone rang and he answered it, his mind already on work, watching distractedly as Cristobel slid off his desk and stood up, smoothing down her tight cream skirt with her hands and pouting at him.

She was moving towards her bag when the door opened and in walked his Spanish-speaking saviour. A number on a file somewhere in the bowels of his cutting-edge glass building, a name he hadn't even been told because it was such an insignificant detail. But that face. The memory of it leapt out at him as though it had been lying just below the surface, nudging the edges of his consciousness.

Gabriel had a moment of utter speechlessness, while Cristobel continued to sort herself out, dabbing some lipstick on her mouth and angling a little compact mirror so that she could inspect her handiwork.

Alex Mcguire. He didn't need Janet to announce her because he realised that he could put the name to the person in an instant, even though it had been years since he had last had anything to do with her. She was as tall as he remembered, as tall as Cristobel was tiny, and she still had that coltish, boyish grace he had once found so unusual and so appealing. Short dark hair, which she had always defiantly refused to grow because she just *wasn't that type of girl*, the type of girl who wore stilettos and push up bras and red lipstick and tight clothes. In fact, he had never, not once, seen her in anything smart, but she was dressed smartly now, in a sober grey suit, although the shoes were still flat and the nails were still short and she still didn't wear much by way of make-up.

Alex, a newcomer to the Cruz business empire, had followed Gabriel Cruz's secretary along the opulent top floor of the offices in a state of nervous tension. At first, when she had been summoned from her lowly office on the first floor, she had steeled herself for a worst case scenario. Had she sent the wrong invoice to the wrong, very important client? Mistyped something critical? Used the wrong tone of voice to the wrong person on the telephone? She might just be a small cog in the finance department, but rumour had it that nothing escaped the mighty Gabriel Cruz's eagle eye and mistakes were never allowed to slip through the net. She needed this job. The salary was so much higher than what she had been getting before and when she thought that she might have blown it by doing something stupid, something that might require a personal summons by the great man himself, then her stomach had twisted into desperate knots and brought her out in a cold sweat.

But then she had been told that she was wanted for her translating abilities and she had relaxed a bit. She could speak Spanish fluently, had been assiduous in maintaining it even though she hadn't been back to Spain for a little over five years. Mr Cruz, she had been told, needed someone to visit the shops with his fiancée because he couldn't possibly spare the time and his fiancée's grasp of English was limited.

Now, as she stared at the legendary Gabriel Cruz, sitting behind his desk, a massive handmade creation which blended various shades of wood and looked as though it cost the earth, she felt the room begin to swim around her. Her throat felt dry, her brain seemed to decelerate to a standstill and a hot, burning tide of horrified colour swept into her face. She had to blink because the sight of the man in front of her was so extraordinarily, terrifyingly unexpected.

Reason tried to push its way through the tangled chaos of her thoughts, telling her that this couldn't possibly be the guy she had known all those years ago, because the guy she had known had not been called Gabriel Cruz and he certainly hadn't been some kind of mega-billionaire, but the testimony of her eyes was telling her otherwise.

She had to take a deep breath to steady herself. But she couldn't look at him. The resemblance was just too uncanny. Maybe it was just seeing this *type*. The sinfully good-looking Mediterranean *type*. Her brain had formed some weird ridiculous link, hence her feeling of being catapulted back in time.

'Well?' Cristobel demanded in Spanish. She looked at Gabriel sourly. 'Is *this* the girl who is supposed to come shopping with me?'

Gabriel was back in control. There was no point in playing catch up games now. 'She speaks Spanish. And, as I have said, I can't spare the time at the moment.'

'Look at her! How is she going to know where to take me?'

'Excuse me?' Alex interrupted, clearing her throat and forcing a polite smile on her face. Did they think that she was a pot plant to be spoken about as though she wasn't in the room? 'If you tell me what sort of stuff you're looking for…' She couldn't bring herself to look at the man lounging indolently behind the desk. Her imagination had been working overtime but she still wanted to get out of that office as quickly as possible.

Any longer and she might just start wondering what would happen if Gabriel Cruz really *was* her Lucio and there was no way that she was going to play mind games with herself and get lulled into visualising how catastrophic that would be.

'I need clothes,' Cristobel snapped. 'I need trinkets for my boxes to go on the tables. I need something exquisite for Vanya.' She moved behind the desk and wrapped her arms around Gabriel. 'And I cannot imagine this girl being able to help me. She has barely said a word since she entered! Darling—' she brushed her lips against his neck and he gently but firmly disentangled her from him '—is there *no one* else in this place who speaks Spanish? I need someone on my wavelength. She doesn't even know how to dress!'

Alex gritted her teeth together. 'I apologise for being a bit lost for words...' she reluctantly allowed her gaze to flit over Gabriel '...but for a minute you reminded me of someone I used to know, Mr Cruz. Sir.' She hurriedly averted her eyes to Cristobel, who didn't look dressed for a shopping trip in the middle of winter. 'I tend to dress in a practical fashion but I know where all the trendy places are.'

'I am not looking for trendy. I am looking for classic.'

'Yes. Well. Those too.'

'I suppose you will have to do. My coat is in the cupboard.'

Feeling as bulky as a bodyguard, Alex fetched the coat and followed in Cristobel's imperious wake, half listening to the further list of things that needed sorting out, half thinking her own thoughts because just seeing Lucio's doppelgänger had opened a door to a bank of memories and now they wafted through her mind, overpowering her attempts at control like a poisonous gas.

Making love to Lucio, laughing, talking until the early hours of the morning and then making love again so that she was exhausted when she rose in the morning to help out in the kitchens where she had been working for part of her gap year. Learning the hotel business while polishing up her Spanish and also developing a healthy tan. And, disastrously, falling in love. Eighteen and in love with the most gorgeous man alive. Boys had always been a known quantity for her. She had four brothers, for heaven's sake! She had known how to relate to them, how to talk about football and rugby and cars. She had even had a couple of boyfriends, drank beer with them and got freezing cold watching football matches in the depths of winter but nothing had prepared her for meeting Lucio. He had been everything a girl could ever dream of, a raven-haired, black-eyed, broodingly and impossibly sexy Spanish alpha male, not a boy but a man and one who had taken her girlish inexperience and turned it on its head.

Five years' worth of uninvited memories were her companions for the remainder of the day and Alex returned to her desk six and a half hours after she had left the office, wrung out and with barely any time to spare. For the first time that day, she succeeded in relegating the disturbing procession of memories out of her head because she was in such a rush to get back to her little terraced house in West London.

She was rummaging in her bag, trying to locate her Oyster card for the underground and save herself the daily embarrassment of holding up a queue of belligerent rush hour office workers while she frantically tried to find the elusive little plastic folder, when her telephone rang and she automatically picked it up, sticking the receiver under her chin so that she could continue her hunt.

Gabriel Cruz's voice, that deep, lazy drawl with its slight foreign intonation, brought her to a screeching halt and she felt her heart speed up. She had done a pretty good job convincing herself that her boss was not a spectre from her past. Gabriel Cruz had never been a broke, nomadic hotel worker. He had always had bucket-loads of money. His family, apparently, could trace their heraldic roots back to the dawn of time. She had managed to elicit that much from Cristobel and the information had finally silenced any lingering fears, but hearing his disembodied voice now made her think that time had somehow managed to rewind, throwing her back to that small hotel in Spain.

'Come up to my office. Now.'

'I'm…I'm sorry. Sir. Mr Cruz. I can't. I'm on my way out. Perhaps it could wait until tomorrow?'

'How long have you been working for my company?'

'Three weeks,' Alex said weakly, glancing frantically between the door and her watch.

'Long enough, in that case, to know that I do not appreciate my employees clock-watching. So that you are crystal clear on the matter—I wasn't issuing an invitation to my office; I was giving you an order.'

'Everything went fine today! I think your fiancée managed to get through most of what she wanted to…'

'In my office. I will give you five minutes.' He disconnected and pushed himself away from his desk. It bugged him that he had not been able to get Alex's image out of his head. He told himself that it was a futile exercise to dwell on what had happened between them. He had enjoyed many women in his life and had never had any problem in relegating them to history once they had ceased to be a part of his life. So why had he found it so difficult to stop thinking about this one? Was it because she had appeared out of the blue and had caught him unawares? Or was it because she held the unique position of having been the only woman he had bedded who had never had an inkling of his material worth? He didn't know. What he *did* know was that she had played havoc with his concentration. He was also keenly aware that thinking about another woman when he was engaged to be married in four months' time was entirely inappropriate.

He drummed his fingers impatiently on the gleaming surface of his desk. It was Friday. It was nearly five forty-five. He had dispatched his secretary, who was accustomed to routinely working overtime. The majority of his employees who occupied the outer offices would have packed up and gone and the remaining directors on the top floor would be ensconced in their offices, cutting deals and making calls until they were summoned home by irritable wives and partners. He should be doing the same. Working. But his brain seemed to have malfunctioned and he had found himself hunting down the company internal directory and then tapping in to Alex's extension because hell, he couldn't allow her to continue to wallow in the illusion that he was a stranger, could he? A stranger who bore a remarkable resemblance to someone in her past! She couldn't really believe that, could she? But, just in case she did, it was his job to disabuse her because she worked for him now and such a delusion would be downright unethical.

When she finally knocked on his door, he found that he was looking forward to their little chat.

'You wanted to see me.' Alex could feel her stomach churning as she hovered indecisively by the door, ready for flight.

'I did.' Gabriel didn't stand. Instead, he sat back and devoted one hundred per cent of his attention to acknowledging how little she had changed. Remarkable. She must be what now…? Twenty-three? Twenty-four? And she still hadn't succumbed to the polish and finesse to which most young people in the capital seemed to aspire. 'Come in.' He gestured expansively to one of the chairs positioned in front of his desk. 'Have a seat. I would offer you coffee but Janet, my personal assistant, has already left.' He shrugged and offered an apologetic smile.

Alex wondered whether a man of his importance was incapable of working a coffee machine. 'I…I really can't stay…'

Gabriel frowned. 'Maybe you didn't quite understand me when I told you that I don't tolerate clock-watching in my employees.'

'I know. And I'm more than happy to work overtime, but I need a day's notice. As it is, I'm already really late for…'

Gabriel raised one imperious hand. 'Not interested. Whatever date you've got lined up will have to wait. There are a few things we need to discuss.' He thought that he had swept all traces of her from his mind but he must have been mistaken because there was a familiarity about her that was strangely disconcerting and he was aware that the faintest colour scored his slashing cheekbones. Déjà vu slammed into him with pulsating intensity and suddenly he could remember everything about her, right down to the smallest details, the tiny freckles across her shoulder blades, the way she always smelt of the pine soap she liked to use, the sounds she used to make when he ran his hands all over her body.

The memories stole into his head like destructive gremlins and he banished them without conscience.

'What things?'

'You said that I reminded you of someone you used to know. Tell me.'

'Wh…what?'

'And stop clinging to that door knob as though you're on the verge of collapse! I told you to sit down!'

Alex could barely hear herself think. The blood was rushing through her and, even though she could see a precipice yawning open at her feet, she was still desperately happy to kid herself that everything was fine. She was having an inconvenient conversation but that was the extent of it.

'I…I really have to go, Mr Cruz. I have…obligations. I know you hate clock-watchers but…'

'I told you. Cancel your date. It'll be a lot easier than you think.'

Alex tried not to look resentful in the face of his implacable smile. In fact, she was trying hard not to look at him at all.

'Okay.' She angled her body away from him and spoke in a low, hurried voice, explaining the situation and lacing her request with a thousand apologies. Then, feeling a bit calmer, she turned to face him.

'So.' Gabriel watched as she gingerly sat down. Her body language was shrieking discomfort. 'This guy you tell me that I remind you of.'

'It's not important. I thought you called me here to find out how my day with your fiancée went.'

'Okay. Shall we use that as our starting point? How did the day go? Feel free to speak your mind. It's something I encourage in all my employees.'

Alex refrained from pointing out that he hadn't much liked it when she had spoken her mind and told him that she had to leave the office. 'The day went very well. She's demanding but I think she got a few things accomplished.'

'Yes,' Gabriel mused thoughtfully, 'I can imagine that you might have found Cristobel a little challenging. What else did you think of her?'

'I don't think it's my place to say, sir.'

'There's no need to keep repeating *sir* at the end of every sentence. So I take it that you two didn't get along…'

'I think she found my translating skills very useful.'

'I'm beginning to get the drift,'

'She's a very…a very…*polished* woman…' She had broken out in a film of perspiration because she suspected that traps were being laid, except she had no idea where the traps were. If she inadvertently stepped on one, would it signal the end of her career? Women, apparently, had a great deal of influence over their men, or so she had read somewhere, and if the mind-numbingly empty-headed socialite Cristobel decided to blacken her name, then she might very well find herself out of a job before she had had a chance to even get her feet under the table. But there was no way that she could pretend a rapport where none had existed. Nor was she finding it comfortable to look at him, which meant that she was addressing her answers to her feet. Hardly the sign of an efficient rising executive in his dynamic company.

An uncomfortable silence lengthened between them until Alex was eventually driven to look up at him and, as their eyes tangled, she felt her skin begin to prickle. The thread of reason that had held sway throughout the course of the day, the notion that there was no way that this man was the same one who had invaded her life and turned it upside down, began to fray at the edges.

When he said softly, 'Would that guy you remember have gone by the name of Lucio…?' Alex barely heard him. His words floated around her head and then, like laser-guided torpedoes, shattered through her protective barriers and her eyes widened in shock and dawning horror.

'How…how did you know?' The truth had already sunk in but, in her determination to block it out, she had subconsciously created all sorts of pointless justifications in her head as to why the guy sitting in front of her, oozing sex appeal and power, couldn't possibly be the Lucio she remembered from years ago. Lucio had been broke. He hadn't descended from the Spanish hierarchy. And surely he hadn't been as tall or aggressive or dangerously masculine as this man?

'I'm surprised you don't recognise me, Alex. I recognised you the second you walked through my door. You know, in a way, I'm a little offended but I'll rise above that.'

'But…but your name's not Lucio…it's…it's…' A great chasm was opening up at her feet and she tried not to stare down into its dark abyss.

'Lucio is my middle name.'

Having laboured to avoid looking at him at all, Alex now felt driven to stare as her memory of Lucio overlapped and merged with the reality of Gabriel Cruz, one and the same person, and of course she had been a complete fool to have thought otherwise. His was not a face to be forgotten, even with the benefit of some serious wishful thinking, and if she had found him good-looking back then, he was scarily sexy now. Time had taken the guy of twenty-six and honed him into staggering perfection.

And he was engaged.

'I don't understand,' Alex stammered in complete confusion.

'What don't you understand?'

'You lied to me? All those years ago? When I saw you in this office, I just thought you resembled the guy I used to know. Why would I think that you had lied to me? I knew someone who didn't have much money and liked the simple things in life. Who *were* you?'

Gabriel's lips thinned and he flushed darkly at the wounded accusation in her voice. She had always been upfront and honest. It had been one of the things he had enjoyed about her. No games, no subterfuge, no hidden agendas. No way was she going to understand his harmless pretence and now he felt like a bastard, which didn't sit well with him because he was someone accustomed to always feeling pretty good about himself.

'I indulged in a piece of innocent fiction,' he drawled with a shrug of his broad shoulders. And it *had* been innocent. Saddled with the weight of responsibility from a young age and already prematurely jaded by the nature of women and the

lengths they would go to in order to fall into the bed of a man
with money and power, the lure of allowing Alex to believe
that he was no more than an ordinary guy who happened to
be working at a nearby fancy hotel, had been irresistible. For
the first time in his life, he had left his gilded cage and tasted
a certain freedom. The vague, nebulous feeling that somewhere, buried deep inside, he had protected that memory,
was something that Gabriel barely registered on a conscious
level. He was not one of those weak men who wasted time
indulging in a load of pointless introspection. He certainly
wasn't going to start now.

'*A piece of innocent fiction?* What's so innocent about lying
to someone?' She was momentarily distracted by the shocking
concept of having been wilfully duped. She had fallen head
over heels with a guy who had thought so little of her that he
had found it okay to spin her a bunch of lies about himself.
How big an idiot had *she* been? 'I believed every word you
told me about yourself!'

'Your memory's playing tricks on you. I never told you
anything about myself.'

'You allowed me to believe that you were an ordinary guy!
You took walks on the beach with me and we ate out at cheap
and cheerful restaurants and you sympathised with the fact
that I was broke and all the time you were actually Gabriel
Cruz, mega-rich and mega-powerful! You played with the
truth and, as far as I'm concerned, that's the same as lying!
You weren't really working at the Tivoli, were you?' On the
fringes of her mind, she knew that this was all irrelevant but
she shied away from confronting her truly ugly dilemma. It
was easier to postpone that by taking refuge in the details of
his deception.

'I was, in a manner of speaking.'

'What manner of speaking would that be?'

'I own the Tivoli Hotel. At least, I do now. At the time, I was in the process of acquiring it.'

Alex's mind reeled. How was it that she had never questioned his self-assurance? His confident charm? The effortless way he seemed to command the space around him? She had just found it unbelievably thrilling. So different from the boys she had known who had seemed like toddlers in comparison.

She wondered whether they had gone to cheap places because he would have been safe from recognition. Rich people wouldn't have been seen dead in cheap tapas bars frequented by local fishermen so the chance of him inconveniently bumping into a fellow millionaire acquaintance would have been nil.

And, hard on the heels of that thought, came another, even more sickening one. She had committed the grave error of telling him that she loved him and he had scarpered. Sure, he hadn't done a midnight flit, but as good as. He had let her down gently, explained that she was young, that they had had fun, that she had her whole life in front of her. He had been immune to her distraught expression and had kindly set her aside when she had clung to him. It had been a sobering experience but over time she had managed to persuade herself that she had had the misfortune to have invested all her youthful love in someone who hadn't felt the same towards her. These things happened. The music charts were littered with singers crooning on about broken hearts and unrequited love.

She was working out now that, even if he *had* been madly in love with her, which he hadn't been, he *still* would have walked out of her life because he was Gabriel Cruz and there was no way he would ever have hitched his wagon to a nobody.

Hadn't she met his fiancée first-hand? Hadn't she seen for herself what he was all about? Rich men needed all the right trappings and that applied to everything, from houses to cars to fiancées. On every level she was waking up to the fact that she had been an even bigger fool than she could ever have imagined possible.

'So,' she said slowly, very, very angry now, 'let me get this straight. Five years ago, you pretended to be someone you weren't *for a bit of fun*. I'm right about that, aren't I? Were you bored with fawning rich girls? Was that it? So you decided that you'd take a bit of time out and pretend to be just like everybody else and I just happened to be the poor schmuck who landed up in your path.'

'You're overreacting!'

'I am *not* overreacting! You may be rich and powerful but that's no excuse to manipulate other people! I *trusted* you!'

'I didn't *manipulate you*,' Gabriel muttered, 'and I didn't do anything with you that you didn't enjoy!' He raked restless fingers through his black hair and Alex followed that graceful movement with a compulsion that terrified her. She didn't want to think about exactly how much she had enjoyed all those things he had done with her.

'That's not the point! The point is, I might have liked having an idea of the person I was dealing with!'

'Why? Would you have behaved differently? Expected a bit more? Five-star hotels, perhaps? Four-poster feather beds and my limo to ferry you everywhere?'

'That's a horrible thing to say!'

'Why is it horrible? Call me cynical, but I've noticed that a healthy bank balance brings out all sorts of predictable behaviour patterns in women.' From the unusual position of self-defence, Gabriel fell back on the dispassionate air of someone delivering self-evident truths.

'Yes, well, believe it or not, there are some women who would run a mile from a man with a *healthy bank balance*.'

Gabriel gave a roar of incredulous laughter, which made her even more furious. 'Really? Let me think about that... No-o-o...don't think I've ever met that particular species...'

'Would you mind telling me why you summoned me here?'

'Why do you think, Alex?' He linked his fingers behind his head and leaned back. 'You don't seriously imagine that you can carry on working for me and kidding yourself that you don't know who I am, do you?'

Alex steeled herself to meet his gaze levelly, without flinching. She was thinking fast now, thinking about all the different ways his reappearance might jeopardize the life she now led, thinking that the last thing she wanted was for him to start picking her out from the herd. It wasn't likely. He was almost a married man. But what if he decided to play catch up games, just for the heck of it? There was too much at stake.

'You're right,' she conceded quietly. 'I shouldn't have... have let my feelings run away with me. It's been a bit of a shock but I'm over it now. You caused me a lot of sleepless nights when you walked out of my life...' she forced herself to smile wryly at him '...but that was a long time ago. It was just an eye-opener hearing the truth about who you were. If I reacted a little over the top, then I apologise...'

Gabriel was watching her carefully, his eyes narrowed. Her volte face was almost as dramatic as her outburst had been. His initial thought was that she was waking up to the fact that there was such a thing as kicking up too much of a fuss. She could reasonably get away with a little, given their past connection, but he was her boss and she was expendable. Hence her strategic back down.

Less welcome was the suspicion that she was trying to get rid of him, but he decided to discard that option.

'Apology accepted,' he drawled, his sharp eyes picking up the way her mouth tightened at that. Sorry, he realised, was something she certainly wasn't feeling.

God, he'd forgotten how feisty the woman was. He'd forgotten how refreshing it had been to be with a woman who didn't tiptoe around him. He'd put into mental cold storage that memory of being able to drop his cynicism and function with an openness he had never had and didn't have now. Crazy, inappropriate memories.

'If that's all, then…?' Alex sprang to her feet and snatched up her bag from where she had earlier dumped it on the ground next to the chair.

It didn't take a genius to figure out that she couldn't wait to get out of his office. Gabriel stood up with his usual lithe, easy grace and strolled over to where she was making a hasty beeline for the door.

'So…' His voice exuded the lazy confidence of a man who expected to be obeyed the second he opened his mouth and, sure enough, Alex paused in her tracks and turned to look at him. 'Where can I find you…?'

'What?' Her face drained of colour. *Find her? Why would he want to find her?*

'I mean, which department do you work for?'

'Why?' Alex asked cautiously.

Gabriel could feel irritation getting the better of him. 'Because I might need your services again,' he told her bluntly. 'Cristobel comes to London on a regular basis. It would be helpful if you could act as her tour guide if I am not available.' Had he meant to say that? Maybe not, but her desperation to get away from him was annoying.

Alex lowered her eyes, cut to the quick. Was he *that* thoughtless that he could suggest some kind of bonding experiment between his ex-lover and his wife-to-be? How thick could one guy get? But then hadn't he proved that his only concern was himself? He had wanted time out five years ago and so he had lied to her and used her. Now, he might need a Spanish translator and so he would demand her services and to heck if she found the arrangement inappropriate.

Put in an impossible situation and already coming to terms with the fact that there was too much at stake for her to remain in her job, Alex raised her eyes to his and ignored the way her pulse quickened as his dark gaze swept over her. She remembered the way he could make her feel. She reasoned that that was why her body felt so tingly, as though she had suddenly become uncomfortable in her own skin.

'That's not going to happen,' she told him quietly. 'I'm not paid to babysit your fiancée whenever she happens to be in London. I also didn't enjoy my duties today. You may be crazy about your fiancée and I'm really happy for you, but there's no way that I'm going to be ordered to go shopping with her again. We aren't similar and we didn't get along. We tolerated each other because neither of us had a choice.' She took a deep breath and found that her hands were shaking so she stuck them behind her back and bunched them into fists. 'Today's been a bit of a shock. It's a weird coincidence that I've ended up being employed in your company but there's no reason why we should have anything further to do with one another. We've both moved on with our lives. I wish you all the best but when I walk out that door, I really don't want to see you again.'

She fled with the last word, even resorting to taking the stairs rather than wait in mounting anxiety for the lift to arrive.

She'd always wondered how things might have turned out had she been able to get in touch with him all those years ago…tell him about Luke. Now he was getting married and his life was in a different place. He had moved on, found the perfect partner. Alex realised that she would just have to accept that there were some waters that could never be disturbed.

CHAPTER TWO

ALEX handed in her resignation the following Monday. There were a lot of questions and raised eyebrows but Alex played it down, using the old time worn favourite about *family problems*. No one liked to ask too many questions when confronted with someone else's *family problems*, especially when the someone else in question had only been employed by the company for less than a month.

She felt a pang of sharp, bitter regret as she quickly and efficiently cleared her desk, but she had had a night to think over the situation and there was no way that she could continue working in the same company as Lucio/Gabriel. He would have had no qualms about ordering her to flit around London with his fiancée, looking at stupid bits of fabric and translating ridiculous questions about shoe colours and flower arrangements. He might even have seen it as fitting punishment, considering she had laid into his wife-to-be with brutal honesty.

She barely gave consideration as to how this development would impact on her meagre finances. She had been too busy making sure that she vacated the smoked glass building with the minimum of fuss and under the radar of Gabriel's eagle eye, should he happen to be around. It was just a stroke of luck that his offices were on the top floor, safely out of harm's way.

One week later and she had managed to land herself back into her old job, which had seemed a miserable step backwards but she could hardly afford to turn the money away. And her old boss had been nice enough about her slinking back with her tail between her legs. No awkward questions. No snide remarks. He had accepted her vague waffle about *things not living up to expectation* and installed her right back into her swivel chair in front of the computer in the small reception area.

Which was where she was precisely eight days later when Gabriel showed up.

She didn't see him. She was busy putting the finishing touches to a document she had been given to edit, racing against time, which was what she always seemed to do the minute the clock struck four-thirty.

From the small corridor, Gabriel's eyes quickly and efficiently scanned the room, for the office was really just one big room, amateurishly divided into cubicles by flimsy partitions. The weather had turned chilly and it was cold. So cold, in fact, that, as his eyes rested on her downbent head, he became aware that she was typing quickly, wearing fingerless gloves and with a woolly hat pulled down low so that only the ends of her short dark hair were visible. The smart get-up in which he had last seen her dressed as she had sat across from him in his office had been abandoned in favour of a pair of jeans and a grey jumper. He guessed that she would be wearing trainers. She had once told him that she had not possessed a pair of high heeled shoes until she turned seventeen and had to attend her grandfather's funeral.

Gabriel wasn't entirely sure why he had attempted this trip halfway across London but she had lodged in his brain like an irritant and he hadn't been able to clear his head of her image.

He had finally persuaded himself that he should see her to make sure that she was all right. She had quit without notice and he had, after all, once been her lover. He felt duty-bound to satisfy himself that she hadn't done anything crazy. She could be impetuous. And she had seemed pretty overwrought the last time he had seen her.

Having successfully attained the moral high ground, he had done the unthinkable and cancelled his meetings for that afternoon, choosing to drive instead to her office, having had someone verify that she was back working there.

It was some minutes before anyone noticed him and then his presence was announced via a network of urgent whispers and giggles until someone who must have been the section supervisor headed towards him.

Alex, he noted with dry amusement, was lost in a world of her own, immune to the flurry of attention his appearance had aroused.

It took no more than a curt nod in her direction to halt the supervisor in her tracks and he felt a moment of gleaming satisfaction as Alex looked up, met his gaze and instantly blanched.

She pulled off the woolly hat and her hair responded by sticking up in little dark spikes before she made an attempt to smooth it back into obedience, standing up and pulling off her gloves at the same time, the focus now of all attention as he continued to lounge indolently in the doorway.

She was red-faced when, after a whispered conversation with her supervisor, she eventually made her way nervously towards him.

'What are you doing here?' was the first thing she said, barely containing her anger.

'Do you know, I had forgotten how tall you were.'

'You haven't answered me!'

'I don't like having prolonged conversations in door-ways.'

'And *I* don't like being hunted down!'

'Why don't we go and discuss this somewhere a little less in the glare of your colleagues? Anyone would think they had never seen a man before.'

They hadn't, Alex thought resentfully. At least not a man like him. She was maintaining a healthy distance and trying to work herself up into an appropriate lather of anger and condemnation but, even so, she was still acutely aware of the power of his presence and the latent strength that vibrated under the veneer of his expensive tailored suit. That she had once known that body as well as she knew her own was just something else that threatened to undermine her defences.

'What do you want?' She glanced at her watch as they walked out into the fading light.

'I want to know why you quit your job.'

'Why do you think?' Alex raised mutinous eyes to his, remembering her old self and how much she had moved on from that place. How much she had been *forced by circumstances* to move on.

'I have no idea. Do I still get to you that much?'

'Don't flatter yourself, Lucio! Or whatever you choose to call yourself!' She turned on her heel and his hand shot out, catching her by her wrist.

'The name is Gabriel. Use it!'

'You're hurting me!'

Gabriel dropped her hand and she rubbed her wrist with her fingers, making a production out of nothing. He hadn't hurt her. Far from it. That feel of his flesh against hers was like having a branding iron planted on her skin. Her whole body was on fire and trembling and *tingling*. Under her jumper and her fleece, she could feel her nipples tighten and begin to throb as they rasped against her lacy bra. It was an appalling reaction.

'So tell me why you quit. Did you have a nostalgic yearning to return to an office where the central heating's obviously broken and the dodgy fluorescent lighting is enough to induce seizures?'

'What does it matter?' But there was resigned weariness in her voice now and she had stopped walking.

As if sensing the shift in atmosphere, Gabriel remained silent and stared down at her upturned face. It was nearly five and the pavements were busy with the usual trawl of workers leaving their offices and kids heading back from after-school activities. He pulled her out of the weaving crowd.

'You were pretty upset the last time we met.'

'Can you blame me?'

'It's been a long time.'

And I can still get under your skin. Alex read that wryly accurate postscript to his baldly spoken statement and blushed, although she didn't say anything, just started walking again, heading towards the bus stop.

'Where are you going? I'll drive you.'

More silence and Gabriel clicked his tongue impatiently. Always alert to the nuances of other people's reactions, he was picking something up now, something unspoken and unsettling. He quickly dismissed that airy-fairy notion as his imagination and instead chose to focus on the surprising fact that this woman from his past, whose image must have been floating really close to the surface of his memory banks because three seconds in her company and he could recall every detail about her, was still affected by him. Why else would she have quit her job? He had done a bit of checking, found out how much more money she had been offered for the post in his company. Walking out on it would not have been the response of someone who had relegated him to the past.

He was only human to have felt a kick of satisfaction at that idea.

'Could you give me a minute, please?' She made a hurried phone call and then turned back to face him.

'Who the hell do you keep calling?' Gabriel demanded irritably.

'Why do you ask? Is it forbidden for someone to make a phone call when they're with you?'

'I don't remember you being so *stroppy*.'

'There's a café just around the corner. If you can't talk in an office, then I can't talk in the middle of the street.' And talking was something they had to do except there was no way that she was going to do, that in his car. It didn't take the intelligence of a genius to figure out which one was his. The office was located in a fairly busy side street but it was by no means a classy area. The parked cars were uniformly serviceable, except for the gleaming black top-of-the-range BMW tucked away between a scooter and a hatchback. She imagined slipping into the passenger seat of his car, with the door shutting firmly behind her and knowing that there was no escape route unless she chose to hurl herself out of the car at forty miles per hour.

Gabriel shrugged but his levels of irritation were rising steadily. He wasn't sure what he had hoped to achieve by descending on her at her workplace but it was beginning to rankle that his reception was somewhat less than warm. He had, after all, only traipsed over out of the goodness of his heart because he wasn't comfortable with the notion that she had quit her job because of him.

'I can understand that you might be a little upset,' he began as soon as a cup of black coffee had been placed in front of him. 'You think that you were lied to…'

'I *was* lied to…'

'You've got to get your head around the fact that the world is a different place for the seriously wealthy.'

'You mean it's a playground,' Alex responded bitterly, staring down into her coffee, which had been stirred into a swirling brown whirlpool. If she shifted just a tiny bit, her knees would touch his and, to avoid that happening, she made sure to tuck her legs to one side. 'You can do whatever you want to do and then sit back and blame the fallout on the fact that you play by a different set of rules.'

'There's no point going over all of this,' Gabriel offered with a slight shrug. 'You deserve an apology and I'm big enough to provide you with one. Does that make you feel better?'

'Why did you bother to come here?'

'To offer you your job back,' he was surprised to hear himself say, although, once the words had left his mouth, he was pretty happy with the decision. Was it possible, he wondered, for a man to be more generous?

Alex looked up at him in surprise and inwardly flinched because just being so physically close to him was like being hit with a sledgehammer.

'Why would you do that?'

'You were being paid twice as much as you're getting at that hole you've thrown yourself back into. Thanks to me—' he let her think about that for a few seconds, happy to take the credit for his magnanimity '—you felt obliged to leave a perfectly good job with excellent prospects and a shed-load of benefits. That situation does not sit well with me.' He took a sip of his coffee and sat back, eyeing her thoroughly over the rim of his cup.

He had always wondered what he had seen in her because she was so unlike the women he had dated. Not just physically, but mentally and intellectually. He was still wondering. The woolly hat and the fingerless gloves had been secreted in the bowels of her oversized bag, but her face was bare of make-up, aside from a bit of mascara and the remnants of some lip gloss. Her nails were unpolished and, sure enough, she was wearing a pair of trainers, which were eminently practical but hideously unfeminine. She worked in an office but she would have looked right at home in the middle of the countryside mucking out. He caught himself wondering what kind of house in the country would suit her, favouring something small and thatched and totally impractical when it came to mod cons, and he nipped his wandering thoughts in the bud.

'In fact, I am willing to up your salary as compensation for the headache.'

'When are you getting married?'

'Come again?'

'Your fiancée didn't mention a date. I think she was too busy being indecisive about the flowers.'

Gabriel frowned. He didn't particularly want to talk about Cristobel. In fact, she hadn't once crossed his mind since she had returned to Spain three days ago.

'March,' he said abruptly.

'A spring wedding. How nice.'

'I didn't come here to talk about Cristobel.'

'How did you meet her?'

'Is it of any importance?'

'I'm curious.'

'I met her at…a party. Something arranged by her parents.' Broadly speaking, it was the truth. He had met Cristobel exactly one year ago and, were he to be brutally frank, he would have described their meeting as contrived, just as he would have described their wedding as arranged. It suited him. His parents were keen for a grandchild and, as his middle thirties loomed, he too felt the time right to get married and settle down. He had played with some of the greatest beauties in the world and tying the knot with someone of equal social standing as himself seemed an acceptable arrangement. He didn't want to think beyond that.

'When did you meet her?'

'This is ridiculous!' He stirred restlessly in his chair and beckoned the waitress across for a refill of coffee. He was irritated to see Alex glance at her watch again. 'I met her a year ago.'

'And was it love at first sight?' One glance at Cristobel had told her that she was just the sort of woman Gabriel would have found satisfactory. Good wife material. And spending a day in the other woman's company had solidified that impression. Cristobel would make the perfect society wife. She had an inbuilt contempt for people who were not of equal social standing and the self-confident, demanding manner of someone whose life has been cushioned by wealth. Alex could see the diminutive, curvaceous blonde rattling off orders in a sprawling mansion in Spain somewhere and bossing around the hired help while her husband worked all the hours God made and multiplied his already shockingly vast fortune on a daily basis.

How strange to think that this was the same guy who had worn jeans and old T-shirts and eaten paella from a plastic plate at a great little café on a beach. She cut short the thought. Right now, he thought all her questions were pointless. Maybe he thought that she was still so consumed with him that she was desperate to know *everything*, even though knowing *everything* was just twisting the knife in an open wound.

Would he die a thousand deaths if he knew how important it was for her to find out about him?

'Where are you going with this?'

'I'm playing the catch up game.' She tore her eyes away from his disturbing, fabulous face and settled her gaze on the less stressful sight of her slowly congealing coffee.

'In that case…' Gabriel leant forward, resting his elbows on the small table and shoving his cup to one side; the sudden closing of distance between them was as dramatic as a blow-torch directed at a lump of wax and Alex instinctively pulled back in alarm '…why don't you tell me a little bit about yourself? For example, why you've looked at your watch six times since we sat down? In a hurry to meet someone?' As far as Gabriel was concerned, this could only signify the presence of a man in her life. Maybe she had to scuttle back to the domestic front to do some vital house cleaning chores. Not for her husband. No wedding ring there and if there was something he knew about this woman, it was that she was nothing if not in love with the idea of romance.

He watched intently as pink colour seeped into her cheeks and felt a sudden, inexplicable rush of anger. So there *was* a man in her life. Why should he be surprised? She might not conform to the stereotype of a beauty, but there was certainly something about her that appealed. Hadn't that something drawn him in all those years ago? Made him forget himself? Made him wonder if sanity didn't lie in overthrowing convention and allowing the unexpected to dictate his responses? In the end, years of ingrained reason had won out.

He wondered what the mysterious guy was like. Obviously no kind of big earner or else she wouldn't have gone shooting back to her averagely paid non-job the second she had walked out of his building. But then, to be fair, money had never been a big deal for her. Still, what kind of guy forced his woman to work at a job she clearly didn't want to do? The picture forming in his head was of someone weak and poorly paid. Who knew? Maybe *she* was the breadwinner!

'Well?' he pressed, keen to find out whether his conclusions were on the right track.

'There *is* someone in my life,' Alex confirmed softly.

Having anticipated a positive response, Gabriel was stunned to find himself at a complete loss for words. He almost wished he hadn't brought up the topic of conversation because what she got up to in her private life was hardly his concern. He had enough on his plate with his own private life and a fiancée who was driving him round the bend with her elaborate wedding plans.

'I'm glad about that,' he said briskly. 'So, about my job offer…'

'I think I'll stay where I am, but thanks anyway.'

'There's no profit in being a martyr, Alex. You obviously need the money…'

'What makes you say that?' she asked with surprise and he pushed himself away from the table, all the better to really look at her. She had, he admitted to himself, the most amazing eyes. Large, dark pools that were once as transparent as glass and full lips that promised laughter. He knew the shape and the feel of her small, high breasts, now totally concealed under her functional jumper. A flash of uncomfortable warmth surged through him and he quickly gathered himself.

'If you didn't need the money, you would have taken your time to find another job. Also, I recognise the trainers. Five years is a pretty long time to hang on to a pair of shoes because you like the sparkly bits on the side…'

Just like that, Alex was catapulted right back to the past, to those glorious, heady days when every single day trembled with promise. It was precisely the last place she wanted to be. She rustled in her bag and fished out her wallet with trembling hands, not looking at him and not caring what he read into her abrupt reaction.

'I really don't think memory lane is appropriate, do you?' she said curtly, pulling out some change and dropping it on the table. 'Considering you're engaged to be married!' She had thrown that at him as a timely reminder, in the hope that he would be stung into retreat, but it had the opposite response.

Instead of embarrassment, Gabriel threw his head back and laughed and, when his bout of amusement had subsided, he said softly, 'You always *did* look very fetching when annoyed. And, speaking of inappropriate, isn't it inappropriate to be jealous when you have someone in your life as well?'

'Don't flatter yourself!' Alex said through gritted teeth, red with anger.

'And there's no need to pay your way.'

'There's *every* need to pay my way!' She knew that she was teetering on the edge of sounding childish but her head felt as though it was going to explode. She just wanted to scream to an unkind fate *Okay, you win! I give up!*

'Your car!' She spun round to look at him and was further enraged to see the traces of amusement lingering on his beautiful mouth. What did he have to snigger about? 'That great big gas-guzzling BMW I spotted outside the office, I take it?'

'Tsk, tsk. Don't tell me you're going to deliver a sermon about global warming.'

'I wouldn't waste my breath!'

Gabriel was enjoying this rampant display of fire. The Alex he had known had been outspoken, yes, but her sharp tongue had never been directed *at him*. Oh, no, in his company she had been all soft and pliant and wonderfully warm and willing. He should have been outraged at most of what she had said to him since their unexpected crossing of paths, but he wasn't. He was intrigued.

'Okay. Hands up, in that case. The gas-guzzling monster is mine.' He beeped it open from a distance and was surprised as she stormed towards it and then stopped dead, with her hand on the passenger door. 'You're asking me for a lift?'

'You offered me one earlier.'

'And you informed me that the bus was good enough.'

'I've changed my mind.'

'In that case, hop in. Give me your address. I'll put it into my sat-nav…' Now he was seriously curious but more than willing to go along for the ride. He wondered if these were delaying tactics before she accepted his wildly generous offer to give her back her job on a silver platter and decided that it probably was. Pride was all well and good, he thought dryly, but it didn't pay the bills. He was slightly disappointed at this pedestrian conclusion to their little meeting, but she would have been a complete fool to have resisted his offer. Especially if she needed to support a half-baked layabout.

'Did you own this when I met you? When you were riding around on a motorbike? Was this in storage somewhere? Having a little holiday while you passed the time of day with the hired hand?'

Gabriel's good mood vanished like dew on a summer's day and his lips thinned. 'Don't put yourself down. I don't like it.'

Alex hadn't realised the depth of her bitterness and was shocked by it. Yes, she still thought about him, which was only natural, but she'd really believed that she had come out the other side of the tunnel. Now a little voice whispered that surely she hadn't. If she had, wouldn't she have found some-one else by now? Moved on? It was what people did after they had learnt their lessons. *He* had moved on. He was on the threshold of getting married! He had moved on *big time*!

She gave him her address and watched as he expertly typed it into the gizmo on his dashboard. She noticed that he hadn't answered her question about whether or not the car had been his when he had been busy pulling the wool over her eyes and decided that it probably hadn't. Didn't really rich people change their cars as frequently as most normal people changed their toothbrushes?

'You were going to go into hotel management,' Gabriel remarked, pulling away from the kerb and glancing across to where she was as still and as stiff as a marble statue. Why had she asked for a lift if he was going to be treated to the silent treatment? he wondered.

'Plans changed.'

'How so?'

Alex twisted so that she was looking at his profile. When he turned and their eyes met, she forced herself not to look away. She was also, she decided, going to make a heroic effort to drop the bitterness, which wasn't going to get either of them anywhere. She had had her say and now was the time to take a deep breath and move on.

'You'll see.'

For the first time, Gabriel felt a twinge of unease. He looked at her but she was staring out of the window. Her neck was long and slender, all the more apparent because her hair was so short, and at this angle the lashes framing her large almond-shaped eyes were long and thick. She had confessed early on in their relationship that she had always been a tomboy, the consequence of having so many brothers. She looked anything but a tomboy, even in her sloppy clothes and the woolly hat which she had stuck back on.

Shockingly, his body kicked in and that shook him so much that he tightened his grip on the steering wheel and applied his mind to the business at hand. The areas through which they drove alternated between cramped and rundown to just cramped until she pointed to a tiny terraced house at the end of the street and instructed him to get parked wherever he could because it was always hell finding an empty slot.

'So you have a car?'

'No. I only go on what I see.'

Her heart was beating fast and hard and nerves had kicked in with a vengeance. She literally felt sick and she had to take a few deep breaths before she opened her car door.

'I'm…I'm really sorry…' she said in a low voice, glancing at him over her shoulder.

'Sorry for what?' Gabriel threw her a sharp look but she was already turning away and slamming the door behind her.

'Sorry for *what*?'

She didn't reply, leaving ample time for him to brood over her enigmatic statement as she yanked off the woolly hat and inserted her key in the lock, pushing open the front door to a flood of light in the small hallway.

Gabriel had a few seconds, during which he took in that it was a bright, welcoming space but small. Much smaller than his place in Chelsea, which was only a two-bedroomed apartment but probably three times the size of her house. There also seemed to be a great deal of clutter. Coats, jackets and various other items of clothing were hung on a coat rack that was groaning under the weight and there was a little collection of shoes which seemed to have started out life in a neat line against the wall but had ended up in a chaotic heap.

Did the guy share the house with her? For some reason, he didn't like that idea.

'Wait here.'

'With the door open? Or am I allowed to shut it?'

'Just wait here and I'll be back in a couple of minutes.'

Gabriel discovered that he was too bemused to argue the toss. He closed the door and leaned against it, his hands in his pockets while he idly scanned the space around him. Yellow walls, a small staircase leading up to what could only be one room, surely, and a bathroom. To his right, the door was ajar and he could glimpse pale walls and the edge of a flowered sofa. Ahead was probably the kitchen and some sort of study, he expected. Not much more.

She returned so silently from a door to the side that he didn't initially register her presence and, when he did, it took him a second or two more before he registered another presence. A kid.

'You never answered my question. Are you going to reconsider my job offer? It's pretty generous, if I say so myself. In fact, I can't think of any other person who would put themselves out to re-hire someone who had walked out of their job for the reasons you gave.'

'Gabriel…this is Luke…'

Gabriel, forced to acknowledge the child, nodded and re-settled his gaze on Alex.

'Mum…can I have some ice cream now? Can I? Susie said I could…'

'Susie said no such thing, you cheeky little monkey!'

From behind him a tiny round girl emerged, grinning as she slung her bag over her shoulder and she ruffled Luke's hair, which produced a little frown before he straightened it.

All of this Gabriel noticed in a daze because his brain had seized upon that one word—*Mum*—and stuck there. He had straightened and was scarcely aware of the enquiring look that Susie directed to Alex before she bustled out of the house.

'Luke, say hi to Gabriel…'

'Only if I get some ice cream.'

'Out of the question, big boy!' But Alex was laughing as she lifted him up and walked towards Gabriel. He looked like a man who had opened an envelope only to discover a letter bomb inside. Alex, on the other hand, was aware of a spreading sense of relief. This had been an inevitable meeting from the very first moment she had stepped into his office and realised that her past had finally caught up with her. She had made a half-hearted attempt to tell herself that things would be better left alone. That Gabriel was engaged, due to be married to a woman he loved and on the brink of starting his own family. That she would be doing him a favour in keeping this secret to herself. She had quit her job, prepared, in the heat of the moment, to just do a runner and deal with the fallout when it happened later down the road. But, time and again, her thoughts had returned to the glaring, naked, unavoidable truth: Luke deserved to know his father, even if it would forever be in the context of a less than ideal situation.

'How was playschool? You're a messy little grub!' He was twisting in her arms now, curious to find out who the stranger in the house was.

Without the benefit of direct comparison, she was only now waking up to the startling physical similarity between father and son. The same dark hair, although Luke's was a curly mop…the same dark eyes…and that olive tint that spoke of his Spanish ancestry. Also that smile and the tiny dimples that came with it. Her heart restricted and she felt a fierce, overwhelming, protective love for her son.

'I'm going to give him a bath and settle him down,' she said quietly. 'You can leave if you want to or you can wait for me in the kitchen. I won't be much longer than half an hour.'

Gabriel could no sooner leave than he could have grown wings and flown through the window. His brain, while taking in everything and already working out a series of consequences, was not functioning at all on another level. He was a father. In what could only be classified as a complete screwup, he was a father, because there was no doubting paternity. Yes, he could make a song and dance about dates and times and then request a DNA test because he was nothing if not suspicious by nature, but the proof of his genetic link to the child was glaringly obvious. He could have been looking at a picture of himself aged four and a half.

He remained frozen to the spot for a few minutes after she had disappeared up the tiny staircase. He was aware of noises drifting down. Very slowly, he made his way to the kitchen and this time, when he inspected his surroundings, it was with renewed interest.

He had a child. And his child was being brought up in conditions that were, if not completely basic, then certainly bordering on it.

He felt the slow build of anger and brought all his formidable willpower into play to stamp on it. From where he was sitting, life as he knew it was over but he would still have to deal with the consequences.

All the paraphernalia of a young child imprinted itself in his head like a tattoo. There was some kind of booster seat gadget attached to one of the kitchen chairs and various plastic utensils on the draining board. He walked across to the fridge and examined the infantile drawings randomly spaced under fruit magnets.

Happy family drawings that ostensibly did not include any father figure.

So there was no guy in her life. When she had talked about her involvement with someone else, she had been referring to her son. *Their* son. He barely deciphered the strangely proportioned pictures he was staring at or the spidery writing underneath. In his head, his eyes were still locked in unwilling fascination on his son's.

There were a thousand questions pounding through his head. In short, he couldn't wait for her to return.

CHAPTER THREE

OF COURSE he wasn't going to leave. Alex had given him the option but she had no doubt that Gabriel would be waiting for her when, after forty minutes, she eventually made her way down the stairs. Luke, sensing tension in the air, had played up, demanding story after story and finally holding her to ransom by extracting a promise of ice cream for the following day before he grudgingly consented to close his eyes.

Without her son as a physical barrier between her and Gabriel, preventing any displays of anger, she felt naked and vulnerable and fairly terrified as she made her way quietly down the stairs to the kitchen.

She reminded herself that she was no longer the impressionable teen she had been years ago when she had fallen under his spell. Then, she would have done anything he asked. She was the puppet and he the puppet master. When he had walked away from her she had fallen to pieces but pregnancy and having a baby, making her way in life as a single mother, moving to London so that she could build a career for herself, which had been nigh on impossible at home, with her family in Ireland, had toughened her up. She might be scared of his reaction but she wasn't going to cower.

Those bracing sentiments were nearly blown to smithereens as she walked into the kitchen to find him sitting on one of the chairs. There was a half drunk glass of orange juice in front of him and he had swivelled the kitchen chair away from the table so that he was facing the door. Waiting for her like an executioner.

'Would you like something hot to drink?' she said, opting for some semblance of politeness before open warfare began. 'Tea? Coffee? Or more orange juice?'

'Is that all you have on offer? What about some whisky? Or gin? I think I'm in need of something a little stronger than tea or coffee.' Faced with the unthinkable, Gabriel could feel himself descending into that unknown territory known as The Emotional Response. It was a route to be avoided at all costs. He had been presented with a problem and the problem would not go away because of his reaction to it.

'I have some wine. It's not very good but it's the best I can do.' Alex poured them both a glass and suggested they sit in the lounge. His silence as they walked there was even more unnerving than if he had been bellowing in her wake. In fact, it sent shivers racing up and down her spine.

'So,' he said once he was seated, 'when were you going to tell me? Or were you going to bother to tell me at all?'

Alex gulped down some wine and then nursed her glass as she stared with a wildly beating heart at the rug on the floor, given to her courtesy of her parents, who had campaigned against her moving to London but, having finally bitten the bullet, had proceeded to kit her small house out with stuff they vaguely labelled *unwanted bits and pieces* but which she knew had been bought new. She visibly jumped when he repeated his question in a voice with icy bite.

'When did you find out?' Gabriel changed tack, enraged by her silence. Was he supposed to feel sorry for her? Her drawn face and miserable, sagging demeanour suggested it but, having had his foundations rocked to their core, his sympathy levels were non-existent. He had never considered the whole issue of children but, when he had, it had been in an abstract way. They would come along at some point in time, as yet undecided. He was engaged to be married but not once had he considered Cristobel as a mother, although he would have been hard pressed to analyse why. If pushed, he would have said that he just wasn't into kids. He would be a father because that would have been the expectation.

Now, faced with the reality of his own child, he was outraged that he was five years late in having any input. During that time, had there been any men on the scene? Of course there would have been! She might not be all curves, but she was as sexy as hell. Any guy with two eyes in his head would see that.

'Well?' he asked in a clipped voice, keeping his unwanted thoughts about other men well to the back of his mind. 'Are you going to answer me or are you going to sit there in silence and expect me to mind read?'

'You're making me nervous!'

'You deserve to *feel* nervous.'

'Why would that be?' She raised angry eyes to him and clenched her hands into tense fists. 'You're the one who did the vanishing act because you didn't want to be tied down to a foreigner you met in passing! You're the one who lied about his identity so that when I found out I was pregnant and tried tracing you I kept running into a brick wall!' Suddenly the room seemed way too small and she stood up and walked across to the window ledge, perching on it and gripping the wood so tightly that her knuckles were white. She felt as though she had to put a little distance between them because the closer she was to him, the less capable she was of thinking rationally. It was like being eighteen all over again and she didn't like the feeling. Being held hostage by her emotions once could be called an excusable error of judgement. Being held hostage by her emotions a second time would definitely come under the heading of suicidal.

'I was nearly four months pregnant when I found out and already back in England. In fact, at university. Thinking that my life could carry on as normal after…after Spain.' She could remember the shock of finding out as though it had happened only yesterday. The dawning awareness that she hadn't seen her period, always erratic, in a while. The home testing pregnancy kit. The horrible feeling of the whole world falling away from under her feet when that telltale little line had appeared. And then everything that came afterwards.

Gabriel flushed darkly. Mistakes, he acknowledged, had been made. Not wilfully, but even so. They would have to be rectified. That was life.

'I tried to contact you.' With a sigh, she resumed her place on the flowered upholstered chair facing him. She couldn't quite meet his eyes so instead she stared at the pattern on the sofa, also flowered. Both generous gifts from her parents, who had dug deep into their savings to help her out. *They* were the ones who had been there for her. Not the guy sitting opposite, who had cleared off with no forwarding address.

'Of course that was impossible.' Her huge brown eyes were bitter. 'I asked at that hotel you were supposed to be working at and they had never heard of a *Lucio*, never mind a *Lucio* with no surname. Hardly surprising since *Lucio* had never existed. I tried describing you, but naturally they would never have put two and two together and come up with the big shot owner of the hotel.'

Guilt found its way through his iron-clad defence system. 'No one could have anticipated this situation,' he said grimly.

'We should have been more diligent with the contraception. More careful.' The Pill had not agreed with her. Instead, they had relied on barrier protection and there had been times when spontaneity had got in the way of common sense. Like a complete idiot, she had airily imagined that there would be no consequences. Her periods had always been irregular. She had vaguely concluded that pregnancy would therefore be less likely than in someone with a tip-top menstrual cycle.

'There is no point going down the *what if* road…' But another stab of guilt penetrated his austerity. At the time, he had told himself that walking away from her had been in her best interests. She had been young, only just out of school, as he had discovered along the way. Definitely not experienced enough to take on or even need any sort of committed relationship, especially with a guy like him. A guy she didn't even really know. She was a free spirit, about to begin her journey through life. He was already marching upwards, an only child programmed to adhere to unspoken expectations.

But, with malign treachery, the image in his head of her, young and frightened, had wormed its way in and was refusing to budge.

'If it is any consolation, I put my hands up and admit that my little white lies may not have been one hundred per cent justifiable.'

'Oh, well, thanks very much for that belated apology.' Alex's voice was laced with sarcasm. She had never been the sarcastic sort. Funny how experience had a way of changing a person.

'My family were very good. I hid out there for a while but in the end I knew that I had to follow the jobs and London was the most likely place for me to get one so I moved in with a friend and then got this place.' She was pleased at how this dispassionate rattling off of the past few traumatic years of her life managed to sound so *ordered* when in fact she had lived in a semi-permanent state of stress and exhaustion.

'And then you happened to run into me.' He was making a determined effort to stay away from the emotive topic of his son being in a house that was barely big enough for one person. This was not going to do. But he would bide his time for the present.

'It was a shock.' She glanced across at him warily. 'You seem to be taking all this very well,' she ventured hesitantly. 'I thought you'd be furious.'

'What would be the point of that?' Gabriel questioned with chilling self-control. 'Would it change anything? My son would still be upstairs sleeping and life as I know it would still have ceased to exist.'

If at any point in time she had daydreamed about a happy-ever-after ending, some surprise meeting which might have concluded with joyous exclamations of love, then those words conclusively put any such fantasy to rest.

For Gabriel, the knowledge that he was a father meant that *life as he knew it would cease to exist*, and since his life had been very happy indeed without either her or their son in it, then he was looking at a bleak future and that hurt. Even after all these years.

'Tell me something,' he said in the same ultra-controlled voice. 'Having quit your job, presumably because running away was the only solution you could come up with, having the dilemma of seeing me again, would you have made any effort to let me know that I was a father if I hadn't sought you out? Or would you have disappeared off the face of the earth and watched my son grow up without my input in his life?'

Alex felt the colour rise to her cheeks. Would she have said anything? She would have years ago, when she had first discovered that she was carrying his child. And she really wanted to think that she was an honest enough person to have done the same now, but he was engaged. In love with another woman. On the brink of settling down and starting a family with Cristobel. She might have grown up over the past few years, but *that much*?

'I see,' Gabriel said softly, reading into her silence.

'You don't understand!'

'Enlighten me.'

'We…we're in different places,' she began weakly. No nod of agreement greeted this remark. She wished his eyes weren't boring into her head. It was disconcerting because, underneath the ice, she could glimpse the seething, passionate core and just thinking about that did strange things to her body. 'I…I've moved on since we knew each other…'

'Moved on how?' Instantly Gabriel was on red alert. *Moving on* was a phrase with which he was well acquainted and it usually indicated from one person to someone else. All of a sudden he was questioning his easy assumption that *the person in her life*, the person to whom she had vaguely referred before this whole bomb had detonated, was Luke. All of a sudden the notion that she might really have met someone else slammed into him with the force of a freight train. 'Is there some guy in your life?' he demanded, leaning forward and resting his elbows on his knees.

'No!'

'Good.' He relaxed fractionally.

'What does that mean?'

'It means that, now I am aware of the situation, a boyfriend on the scene would be entirely inappropriate.'

Alex felt a red mist of anger envelop her like a cloud, smothering all her good intentions to keep things cool, composed and adult. If she had had something heavy and breakable to hand, she would have flung it at his deceitful, arrogant head and hang the good intentions.

'Would you mind repeating that?' she asked in a tight, unnaturally high voice.

'No man on the scene.'

'No. Man. On. The. Scene. And yet it's all right for *you* to have a *fiancée* on the scene, is it?

What were his expectations here? she wondered. Carry on with his life, get married and lock her up in a state of permanent celibacy because he didn't want another man around his son? She was trembling with anger.

'You're overreacting.'

'I am *not* overreacting!'

'I am being honest. Isn't that what you would want? The truth? And the truth is that I would not welcome anyone else having an influence over my son. What's so difficult to understand about that?'

'I don't want to talk about this,' Alex said tightly. 'I don't want to get into an argument with you. Now that you know about Luke, we can try and sort out…the practical stuff…'

'Does he know who I am?'

'No. I haven't told him yet.'

The enormity of their situation struck Gabriel forcibly at that bald statement. He had an instant picture in his head of his son, all black curly hair and big drowsy eyes, and from nowhere sprang a crazy, confused feeling of time wasted.

'I'm sorry,' Alex said quietly, at which his expression became shuttered once again.

'When do you intend to tell him?'

'As soon as possible.'

'Try again.'

'Okay! Tomorrow! I'll tell him tomorrow! He's very inquisitive, anyway. He'll probably wake up with a hundred questions about you.' Her eyes skittered from Gabriel to the window behind him to the mantelpiece, on which sat a row of pictures of Luke at various stages of his young life. Gabriel followed her eyes and he slowly stood up and moved across to the mantelpiece, where he proceeded to hold and examine all of the pictures. All seven of them. From infancy to the one she had taken last month.

While he had been blithely pursuing his goals with the relentless drive that came so naturally to him, while he had been adding to his fortune, building his empire and congratulating himself on his well run, well oiled, no-unpleasant-surprises-life, his own flesh and blood had been growing up without him around. Frustration rocked him because it wasn't as though he could blame her. Of course, she might have been lying. She might have never bothered trying to find his whereabouts, but he seriously doubted that. He would have been an instant and permanent meal ticket. Why would she have turned that down? He replaced the last of the photos and turned slowly round to look at her.

'When are you going to…tell the people that you know? Your family? Your fiancée?' she said awkwardly, to cover the silence.

'Immediately.'

She breathed a little sigh of relief. Once that hurdle was over, once the shock was absorbed and the situation accepted by the people who mattered to him, they would be able to discuss arrangements for him to see his son. She wondered how Cristobel would receive the news. Not well, she anticipated, but it was hardly as though he had been unfaithful.

'Then, maybe, when you've done that…well, and I will have told Luke about you, of course…we can try and sort stuff out…'

'*Sort stuff out…?*'

'Yes. You know. Visiting rights. I'm really happy for you to see Luke whenever you want to…' She had stood up in preparation to seeing him to the door but now her voice trailed off because he wasn't saying anything. And he was looking at her as though she had a screw missing. And neither of those things added up to a man on the verge of departure, having settled matters.

'*Visiting rights?*'

Alex detected the odour of a trick question and she looked at him warily. 'Yes? Visiting rights? You come to see Luke and take him somewhere for an afternoon?'

'You don't really think that that's going to work, do you Alex?'

'Not going to work?' Alex repeated in dumb founded confusion. 'Why wouldn't it work? It's what everyone else does when their relationship falls apart and there's a child involved. Not that we ever *had* a relationship.'

'Since when am I *everyone else*?'

She was struggling to get the gist of what he was saying but her mind wasn't obliging. Had she misread all the signs and signals? Was he implying that his intention was to stroll out through her front door and disappear over the horizon without a backward glance at his son? Since that seemed highly implausible, she settled on the other, more likely option. He was engaged, he had his life in order. He didn't need a murky, unwanted past misadventure rising up to wreak havoc with his perfect life and so he would keep it a secret.

'I don't intend Luke to be hidden away!' She sprang to her feet, shaking, her hands on her hips. 'He deserves better than that! So, if that's the road you're going down, then you'd better clear off! I can't believe this. I really, can't, Lucio! Gabriel!'

'Sit down!'

'Stop giving me orders when you're in my house!'

'Then stop behaving like a child!' Gabriel had no idea what she was talking about and he recognised that she was in a pretty hysterical frame of mind. She thought he was a louse and, while he was prepared to concede some mistakes made on his part, they were mistakes only in retrospect and only in view of the current extraordinary circumstances. While he was, once again, dealing with the unique temptation to lose his temper, he noticed that she was no longer shouting. Like a burst balloon, she seemed to have suddenly deflated. Her shoulders were slumped and, as he stood up and approached her, he could see tears leaking from the corners of her eyes.

She wasn't a crier. She'd once told him that crying was for small, dainty girls, that tears just didn't suit her. Even when he had walked away from her *for the best possible reasons*, she had been distraught and her eyes had filled up and her lips had wobbled but she had managed to hang on to her self-control. So to see her so utterly crushed did something to him.

'Why are you so good at making me feel so bad?' he murmured half to himself, reaching into his pocket and extracting a pristine white handkerchief. He didn't think she had heard him but once the words were out of his mouth, he realised that no truer ones had ever been spoken because, lurking just below the surface, just beyond the reach of consciousness, there had always been the unpleasant suspicion that he had not behaved properly towards her. Seeing her again had brought all those hidden feelings rushing to the top.

He pushed the handkerchief into her hands and then, still working on automatic, he put his arms around her. It was electrifying. His mind cleared of everything but the sensation of her against him. It was hauntingly familiar, from the length of her to the slenderness of her boyish frame. Her breasts, small and rounded and soft, pressed against his chest and he was overwhelmed by a suffocating desire to shove up her top and slide his hands underneath her bra so that he could caress her. The swiftness of his response, almost as though his body had been waiting for just this moment for a very long time, galvanized him into action and he released her abruptly and turned away.

Alex sniffed into the handkerchief, missing the sudden lack of warmth while cursing herself for having disintegrated like a fool in front of him.

'What sort of man do you think I am?' Gabriel demanded, sinking into the chair, half conscious of his inappropriate arousal. 'What would give you the idea that I intend to keep my own son out of sight?'

'You're not interested in visiting rights.' Alex blew her nose and subsided back into her chair. For once, she wished that she was blessed with long hair so that she could let it fall against her face like a silky curtain, blocking out her weepy, puffy eyes and blotchy skin. 'Which means that you're not committed to seeing Luke. I realise that all this must be a terrible shock for you, but…'

'Stop trying to second guess me. I intend to take my responsibilities head on. I won't be abandoning my own son because he doesn't happen to fit in with my lifestyle. But you're right. It's a great shock and it will be an enormous upheaval.' He sighed heavily and ran his fingers through his hair.

'It's not as bad for you as it could be,' Alex said with a stab at optimism.

'Run that by me?'

Her eyes tangled with his dark, piercing gaze and she felt her bones turn to water. This was precisely the sort of out-of-control feeling that she had to stop.

'I'm sure Cristobel would understand. I mean, it was something that happened before you met her! In fact, chances are that she'll feel sorry for you.'

'Really? I'm not seeing it.'

Frankly, nor could Alex but, before she could plough on with her upbeat approach, he raised his hand to silence her.

'I will naturally have to announce this situation to the world,' he said heavily. 'Starting with my parents.' He imagined their disappointed faces. They had both seen it as their mission to marry him off and the upcoming wedding had been planned meticulously for months. He had distanced himself from as much of the tedious detail as he could get away with, but he still knew that his parents were like a couple of kids on Christmas Eve with their excited preparations and never ending lists of people to invite.

'Then there is Cristobel. There is no question that the wedding will have to be called off.'

For a few seconds, Alex wondered whether she had heard correctly and she stared at him with a blank, uncomprehending face.

'What are you talking about?' she asked in genuine bewilderment.

Gabriel wondered whether she could really be that naive. Hadn't she already clocked that, by detonating her little hand grenade, she was, in passing, doing herself a massive financial favour? A quick glance around him was enough to confirm that hers was a life devoid of any luxury.

'You don't think that I would really agree to have my son brought up in these conditions, do you?'

'These *conditions*? There's nothing wrong with where we live! Have you any idea how hard I've worked to be able to afford this place? Even with Mum and Dad having to help out now and again?'

'Yes, and here's where I come in. You can start relaxing.'

Having digressed, Alex brought the conversation back to its origin and again asked him what he meant by having to call off his wedding.

'I have a child and no child of mine will be raised illegitimate. Connect the dots, Alex.'

'Are you asking me to *marry you*?'

'I don't see all that many choices staring me in the face, do you?'

Alex felt the weight of pain settle in her chest like a rock. Five years ago, she could have thought of nothing better than to receive a marriage proposal from this man. She would have abandoned all thoughts of a university career without a backward glance. Now here he was, years down the road, proposing marriage because he could think of no other choice, given the situation in which he had found himself dragged. Did he expect her to feel *grateful*? She sincerely hoped not because gratitude was way down the list of things she was currently feeling.

'Okay. So let me get this straight. You would break off your engagement to Cristobel, dump all your wedding plans to marry me because I happen to be the mother of a son you never knew you had.'

'Like I said. Not too many options staring me in the face.' Gabriel was surprised to find that he felt a lot less disturbed at this eventuality than he would have expected. Why was that?

Never given to the pointless luxury of introspection, it crossed his mind that his choice to marry Cristobel had perhaps been the result of silent pressure from his parents and a general logical awareness that marriage was the next step. Cristobel ticked all the boxes and she had been more than eager to oblige. On paper, it had had everything going for it. Until now. On paper, this arrangement he was proposing not only made more sense but was, in fact, a necessity.

'We'll have to get it done sooner rather than later,' he mused, thinking of his parents and bracing himself for the inevitable ugly fallout. 'My parents will doubtless be disappointed at the turn of events but knowing that we have married and given my son the Cruz surname should go a little way to easing the situation.' He thought that Cristobel would be a rather different matter. And then there were all those wedding arrangements to un-arrange. And the further hassle of press intrusion. Like it or not, his was a public face. He would have to act swiftly to avoid even the merest whiff of a scandal.

'I could arrange something quiet for the weekend.' He glanced quickly at his watch and frowned. 'Once that's out of the way, we can go somewhere abroad until the fuss dies down. Naturally, I will only be able to be with you for a very short while. It would be impossible to leave my business concerns for too long...'

'I don't believe I'm hearing this.'

'I know.' Gabriel's mouth twisted into a dry smile. 'You must find it almost beyond belief that you've managed to hit jackpot. Who would have thought it?'

'I have no intention of marrying you.'

'You really don't mean that,' Gabriel said patiently.

'No, but I really *do*,' Alex said, her pulse leaping with anger and loathing. 'First of all, we're not living in the Dark Ages. *You* might think that sacrificing your life because of some warped sense of family honour is the thing to do, but *I* don't. *Secondly*, Luke deserves more than the two of us trapped in a loveless marriage!' She could see his face becoming more coldly disapproving by the second but there was no way that she was going to be browbeaten into doing something that was all wrong. 'Do you really imagine that I'm so pathetic and desperate that I would accept marriage to you in these circumstances?'

'Wasn't it the thing you wanted most when we were to-gether?' Gabriel said with cutting smoothness.

'That was *years* ago! Believe it or not, I'm a different person now!'

'How different?' Gabriel murmured and, just like that, Alex could feel the atmosphere between them subtly alter. His eyes did a lazy sweep of her body and came back to rest on her flushed face. That kick of awareness that had sprung from nowhere earlier on resurged back into life. He had a rich, graphic fantasy of taking her to bed again, feasting on the body the way he used to. He wondered how pregnancy had changed it and the craving to satisfy that curiosity hit him swift and hard.

So wouldn't that be a great bonus to the whole sorry situation? he wondered. If he was to be married to her, then why shouldn't sex play a part in its success? As if his imagination had suddenly been given the green light, the urge to take her was more powerful than anything he had known before and, why kid himself, it had been there the second he had seen her in his office. He shifted uncomfortably in his seat and tried to focus.

Alex looked at him and fought against the tingly feeling she was experiencing, as though she were being intimately caressed, even though he wasn't even near her. 'I think it's time you went home, Gabriel and gave some thought to how we're going to deal with this *in a realistic way*.'

'This is a supremely realistic way of dealing with the situation.'

'Not for me, it isn't.'

For the first time, it was beginning to dawn on him that his marriage proposal might truly have met with a negative response. Her lips were tightly pursed and her tilted face smouldered with stubbornness. What the hell, he thought, was the problem here? Hadn't he just done the most decent thing possible?

'I don't intend to be shackled to someone who would rather be somewhere else,' Alex continued, just in case he wasn't getting the message.

'This isn't about you; it's about our child.'

'A child you don't even know!'

'Naturally, getting to know him will take time.'

'Good. I'm glad you said that,' Alex inserted quickly, thinking on her feet, 'because that should be your first step.'

Gabriel frowned. 'First step?'

'Get to know Luke. Take him out. Incorporate him as part of your life. It's not going to be easy. You've suddenly found yourself landed with a four-year-old child and you have zero experience of children…'

Gabriel's sharp brain moved rapidly on to another track. 'Of course. And what are the other steps in this realistic scenario of yours?' he asked with a slow smile that sent shivers racing through her. 'Should I do the modern day thing and proceed with my marriage plans?' There was no chance of that but he allowed a few seconds of silence, during which she might contemplate that alternative route. 'Needless to say, Cristobel, as my wife, would have enormous input into all decisions taken regarding Luke. How do you feel about that?'

Not good, was the first thought that came to Alex's mind. She didn't like the thought of Cristobel being any kind of role model for her child. Complicating the scenario came a sneaking thought: sharing Luke with Gabriel was one thing, but what if he wanted more of his son somewhere along the line? She blanched and cleared her throat.

'And naturally my parents would want involvement as well. They live in Spain. It's possible that there might be occasions when Cristobel would take him across for holidays…'

'Holidays?'

'So tell me how you see things working out…. Sell it to me.'

Alex threw him a venomous, trapped look from under her lashes. 'How do you think I feel, knowing that you would ditch the woman you love just because mistakes were made years ago and I got pregnant as a result?'

'I know how you *should* feel.' He had no intention of getting wrapped up in some caring, sharing, ridiculous conversation about his feelings for Cristobel. If Alex was finding it hard to appreciate the enormous generosity of his gesture with her, then she would be at a complete loss to understand a marriage that might have been more of a suitable arrangement than a match made in heaven. 'You *should* feel a certain amount of respect for a guy who's willing to do the right thing. Not many would.'

Alex wondered in confusion how she had managed to turn into the *bad guy*.

'And you should feel a certain respect for a woman who's willing to turn down a wedding ring and an easy lifestyle because she has principles! Not many would.'

Gabriel's steely control slipped and he was subjected to a rush of aggressive anger. Where was she coming from? What airy-fairy planet did she inhabit? But, then again, out of all the women he had ever known, she occupied a unique spot and not just because she was the mother of his child. She was feisty and her failure to be impressed by money was staggering. The harder he pushed for what he wanted, for what he considered *inevitable*, the faster she would retreat. But he *would* get his own way. He always did and he wasn't going to break the habit now.

CHAPTER FOUR

THE first Alex knew of what was happening behind the scenes was when she opened her newspaper three days later, as usual scanning the headlines and then sitting down to relax with the gossip pages in the centre. This was her favourite time of the day. Seven-thirty. Luke safely tucked up in bed, having, as usual, cunningly contrived to keep her reading bedtime stories to him for as long as possible. Small glass of wine on the table next to her and the television turned on but with almost no volume because, whilst she liked the comforting background noise, she wasn't too interested in what the noise was actually about.

It irked her that since everything had come out in the open with Gabriel, she had been able to think of nothing else but him. He hadn't contacted her. On day one she had assumed that the shock of the situation had driven him into a temporary retreat, time out to consider his options and think about what he was going to do next. But now, after three days of silence, she was beginning to think that he had simply chosen to disappear.

Which, she told herself repeatedly, meant no change for her. He hadn't been on the scene for the past five years and so the fabric of her life would remain exactly the same. She also told herself repeatedly that it was just as well that Luke was none the wiser that the stranger who had appeared and then just as quickly disappeared had been his father.

In fact, to count even more blessings, wasn't she glad that she had reconnected with him? Put to bed all those haunting *what if* and *if only* scenarios which had continued to jostle around in some weird Pandora's Box in her head, clamouring for a hearing? Wasn't it *healthy* that she had finally seen him for the person he really was? A man who had knowingly deceived her. He'd disappeared from her life because she hadn't been good enough for him, hadn't been like the Cristobel airhead to whom he was now engaged. He was a guy who made all the right noises when confronted with a difficult situation but then scarpered as fast as he could the minute he was through the door. In other words, a fully signed up, one hundred per cent member of the Creep Club.

The fact that he was still managing to get under her skin and give her, *yet again*, sleepless nights infuriated her.

And her low level, never-quite-gone-despite-all-efforts fury was seething just below the surface as her eyes fell on the hot gossip headlines in the tabloid which announced the end of the perfect engagement between *billionaire whizz-kid Gabriel Cruz and Cristobel Rivera, daughter of import/export magnate Geraldo Rivera*. It took Alex a few stunned seconds before she could read and then reread what was clearly being touted as the scandal of the year. She even had to switch off the television so that she could concentrate on the article, which carried on over the page, and also stare at the photograph of the tiny blonde scurrying away from the limelight wearing a pair of oversized designer sunglasses and shielding her eyes from the intrusion of, presumably, a barrage of cameras. Another photo depicted Gabriel dressed in a suit and looking unruffled at the chaos his announcement had provoked. Typical.

There was an awful lot of background information on the ditched fiancée, which only proved her eligibility for a guy like Gabriel. Moneyed background, at home in the playground of the Rich and Famous, as opposed to the playing fields of the Hard Working and Almost Always Broke. And there was wild speculation as to what could have generated the break up but, even on a fourth reading, Alex could find no mention of either herself or Luke.

The shriek of her mobile interrupted a compulsive fifth reading of the article and Alex nearly spilt the glass of wine in her shaking hand.

Even before she heard his voice, she knew that it would be Gabriel. It was as if her antennae had been put on to red alert and primed for his presence in her life.

'Sitting down, I hope?' he enquired in a silky voice that made her glance furtively around just in case he happened to be hidden somewhere in the vicinity and could see the reaction his voice had on her mangled nervous system.

'I...I've just read...'

'I thought you might have.'

'You...should have warned me that...'

'You had all the warning you needed. I told you that I would be breaking off the engagement. You must have known that it would hit the news. I'm a public figure, whether I like it or not.'

'Yes, but...'

'You can hold that thought. I'll be over in forty minutes. It would probably be better if I used a back door. Is there one?'

'Use a back door?' Alex was fast remembering the past few days of silence, during which her entire life had been turned on its head as she tried to find ways of reconciling herself to his disappearance. She felt as though she was now destined to start the endless cycle of highs and lows all over again.

Just like that. He had walked back into her life and instead of finding her defences in place, she had discovered a gaping lack of body armour. *'Use a back door?'* she repeated in a higher voice. 'You're not playing the lead in a spy thriller, Gabriel! And yes, I have a back door and you're more than welcome to use it but you'll still have to get to the front of the house first because it's at the side!'

'Are you in a mood because I haven't been in touch for the past couple of days?'

'I'm not in a mood.'

'Good. Then I'll see you shortly.'

Alex was treated to the sound of the dial tone as he rang off and she glared at the phone for a few seconds before springing into action. The constant frustrating whirlpool of nagging, unwanted thoughts about Gabriel was replaced by a frantic rush of blood to her head as she scrambled upstairs, changed out of her sloppy jogging bottoms and baggy T-shirt into a pair of halfway decent jeans and a short-sleeved checked shirt that nipped in at the waist and ran her fingers through her hair.

Her cheeks were flushed and her eyes were over-bright. It shouldn't have mattered what she wore but his disparaging remark about her house not being good enough for his son still rankled. As did the fact that she knew, without a shadow of a doubt, that the remark also applied to *her*. House too average for his son, and ex-girlfriend way too average for him.

She was in a fighting mood by the time the doorbell rang forty-five minutes later and she swung to open the door, making a great show of checking the road behind him.

'Phew. Doesn't look like you've been followed. Maybe you'd better sneak in, just in case.'

'Hilarious, Alex. Just open up and let me in.' Gabriel couldn't help himself. His eyes darkened as they took in the tight faded jeans and the small plaid shirt with the top two buttons undone so that just the shadowy promise of breast was visible.

The past few days had been fairly hellish but, even so, he was feeling pretty good about life in general. As he would, he had smugly acknowledged, doing the right thing as he was.

Cristobel had been a nightmare and he couldn't blame her. She had watched her future crash and burn and he had offered nothing by way of a reasonable excuse. Time enough for the situation to be explained in its entirety. Instead, he had attempted some consolation by pointing out their fundamental differences and informing her that she would be well rid of him. He didn't love her. She didn't love him. When she had shrieked that *there was more to marriage than love*, his mouth had tightened, even though she was preaching to the converted. After all, wasn't he the prime proponent of that theory?

He had left her apartment with the peculiar feeling that he had been given a reprieve. What would this woman, perfect on paper, have been like as a wife? She had grown from a rich, indulged girl to a rich, indulged woman and it wouldn't have been long before she became a spoiled, dissatisfied spouse, intolerant of anyone outside her gilded social circle. How was it that he had never seen that promise before?

Surprisingly, his parents had taken the news well, although it had been hard to tell from the other side of the Atlantic and on a phone link. He would fly over very shortly, he had told his mother. Speak with them face to face. But certainly, at the moment, he realised that he had allowed a situation to develop that would not have been right in the long-term.

'Your mother would probably agree with you, son,' his father had said in a low voice. 'Although this is between us men. She always had her reservations about Cristobel. Nice girl, I am sure, and of course it certainly would have made for a powerful merger, but, let me put it this way, do not feel as though you are disappointing us…'

Gabriel had not known whether to believe that statement or if it had just been his father putting a brave face on things. But now, he at least felt as though he was starting with a clean slate.

'You *could* have told me what to expect.' Alex stood back from him and folded her arms, thereby providing some much needed protection against the brutal power of his presence.

'Is Luke asleep?'

'Of course he is. I have very strict guidelines about his bed times.' This just in case he got it into his head that she was a bad mother.

'Stop playing the injured party.' Gabriel swept past her, divesting himself of his jacket in the process and slinging it over the banister. He went straight to the kitchen, opened the fridge and proceeded to help himself to a glass of wine while Alex trailed behind him and gaped at the high-handed way he had just *made himself at home*.

'Why didn't you get in touch?'

He looked at her over the rim of his glass and a slow smile curved his mouth. 'You sound like a nagging wife. Why? Did you miss me?'

'Like a severe case of flu!'

Gabriel threw back his head and laughed. 'I had forgotten your quirky sense of humour.'

Alex watched him with seething resentment. 'I'm glad you find this situation such a bundle of laughs, Gabriel.'

'Let's get one thing straight right here and now…' He deposited his glass on the small pine table and leaned against the kitchen counter and looked at her grimly. 'This is the least amusing situation I have ever found myself in and if you think you can stand there, fuming and behaving as though you're due the sympathy card, then think again. *I* am the one whose life has come to a grinding halt! *I* am the one now faced with a series of decisions which will affect the lives of more than just myself! *You* behaving like a brat isn't going to help matters! Am I making myself understood loud and clear?'

Alex stared down stubbornly at her feet, acknowledging that there was more than an element of truth in what he was saying but still resenting his tone of voice.

'I never asked you to change your life for me,' she mumbled indistinctly.

When she raised her eyes, it was to find that he had pushed himself away from the counter and was towering above her. She wished she had worn heels instead of a pair of socks. At least, with the benefit of heels, she would have been more or less on eye level with him.

'I'm not changing my life for *you*,' Gabriel ground out. 'I'm changing my life for my son.'

You mean nothing to me. That was the implied, unspoken rider to his statement, Alex thought. He intended to do the right thing for his son and in the process she would be dragged along, whether she liked it or not. He couldn't have reminded her more forcibly of his take on events than if he had printed a sign saying *you're someone I happen to be stuck with* and shoved it in her face.

She took a deep breath. 'Maybe we should talk in the sitting room. I…I haven't eaten dinner yet. There's a casserole in the oven. It could just about stretch to two.'

It was an olive branch of sorts and Gabriel knew better than to snap it in two. But her stubbornness did things to his normally cool head that he wouldn't have thought possible.

'I thought you hated cooking.' She had worked in a hotel to practise her Spanish but she had once confessed that kitchens made her dizzy. All those items of food and ingredients in bottles baffled her. He wanted to smile at the memory.

'I've learnt…to…I prefer to give Luke home-cooked food,' she said reluctantly. 'I can manage a casserole but anything fancier than that is out of the question.'

'So he's yet to sample a soufflé…'

Alex dipped past him towards the sitting room at the front of the house. She knew that this polite banter was his way of making the best of a bad situation and she would have to go along for the ride or else make life a constant battleground for them both, and inevitably for Luke. She couldn't do that. But dredging up memories of their brief shared past was more than she felt she could handle. Yet where was the common ground between them now? They were operating in an unreal space, where the normal rules of social engagement were suspended.

'What happens now?' she asked abruptly, as soon as they were sitting. Gabriel on the sofa, she on the comfy chair by the fireplace. Her half finished glass of wine was still there and she took a sip but it had gone warm.

'I didn't see any mention of Luke in that article…' she carried on, drawing up her long legs and then resting her chin on her knee.

'Because I didn't mention him. There was no point getting into the nitty-gritty and, besides, I have little respect for reporters. The world will find out about you both when I'm good and ready.'

'You mean you haven't told your fiancée *the truth*?'

'*Ex*-fiancée. And no. Time enough for that.'

'What on earth did you tell her?'

Gabriel shrugged. 'I told her that ours was not a relationship that was destined to last the course and, as such, we should break it off before we both made a mistake.'

'That little speech should have come easy to you, Gabriel. You must have had years to practise it.'

Gabriel looked at her broodingly. There would be no profit in taking up this futile conversational thread. His mission was to get her on board and the only way he could do that was via dialogue. 'Cristobel will have no trouble in finding my replacement.'

'That's not as easy as you think!' The words were out before she could do something useful, like swallow them back and give herself a stern reprimand for even going there. There was a thick, pulsating silence, during which Alex could feel the slow crawl of embarrassed colour into her face.

'What are you trying to say?' he murmured in the sort of lethally sexy undertone that had always been able to send her pulses skyrocketing into the stratosphere. 'That I'm still on your mind?'

'Of course not!' Alex shot back wildly. Their eyes met and, for a brief moment, she could feel her senses go into agonised, melting free fall. With a sense of deep mortification, she was aware of a dull ache between her legs and the tickle of dampness that proved the effect he was having on her.

'Because it's nothing to be ashamed of…I still happen to find you a very attractive woman…'

'How can you sit there and say something like that when you've only just broken off your engagement? How fickle *are* you?'

In the space of a heartbeat, Gabriel could feel the tables turn on him. She seemed to have developed a talent for doing that. From nowhere, she could generate an argument of ridiculous proportions. 'I was never in love with Cristobel,' he heard himself say and then immediately wondered why the hell he had felt the need to justify himself. Since when did he ever do that?

'You weren't in love with her?' Her heart skipped a beat and she put that down to her surprise at his flat, unvarnished statement. She also had a moment of pure elation and she put *that* down to the fact that, without love in the equation, there would be a lot less to feel guilty about. And wasn't that cause for elation? Her life had suddenly become so complicated that any help in reducing her stress levels was a reason to celebrate!

'No, I wasn't in love with her, Alex,' Gabriel said heavily, frowning at her disapproving expression. 'You should feel better because of that,' he pointed out through gritted teeth because he seemed to have lost the reins of the conversation, which had been going very nicely. 'You weren't responsible for destroying the love match of the century.'

'Why were you going to marry her?'

'Why is any of this relevant?'

'You should never answer a question with a question.' Alex smirked. 'I distinctly remember you telling me that once.'

Gabriel threw his arms up in a gesture that was exotically foreign and muttered an oath under his breath. 'It was a union that made sense,' he offered.

Obviously the wrong choice of words because she looked at him squarely and then mused, '*A union that made sense. A bit like what you had in mind for us…*'

Gabriel opened his mouth to correct her on using the past tense when it was very much still his current intention to settle upon his son the mantle of legitimacy, whether she liked it or not, but he decided to steer clear of reminding her of that.

'I hope you appreciate the fact that, as yet, neither you nor Luke have been mentioned…'

'Remind me why I should appreciate that?'

'Because I don't suppose you'd want the paparazzi camping on your doorstep.'

Alex could feel her brain lagging behind. She was still caught up in the fact that he would have approached marriage as a sensible business arrangement. Proof that there was a block of ice where his heart should be, was fairly piling up.

'You never used to be so *cold*,' she said, thinking aloud. 'I mean, unless you hid it really well.'

'You've lost me.' Gabriel flushed darkly and scowled. Thinking back to those heady times with her was like remembering a different person. He hadn't strolled on a promenade eating an ice cream cone since he had been with her. Incognito. Being Lucio had been a far cry from being Gabriel Cruz. Unfortunately, this was his life. Promenade strolls eating ice cream and pretending the world as he knew it didn't exist had been enjoyable but it was a thing of the past. And being reminded of that served no purpose. Nor did he care for the implication that he was some kind of soulless monster because he happened to take his responsibilities seriously.

Nor, for that matter, did he care for the expression she was wearing on her face, which seemed to be a combination of incomprehension and pity.

'Have I?' Alex asked, staring off into the distance before settling her thoughtful gaze on his face.

'But all this is by the by. I haven't come here for a character assessment, Alex.'

'No. Well, I'm hoping you haven't come here to repeat your offer of marriage because I haven't changed my mind. Cristobel,' she added for good measure, 'might be prepared to enter into a loveless business arrangement with you because the perks are good, but I'm not.'

'Whoever mentioned anything about marriage?' Gabriel shrugged. 'I offered to do the decent thing; you turned me down because you'd prefer to occupy the moral high ground.'

Alex was disconcerted to discover that she was vaguely disappointed at his rapid retraction of his marriage offer. 'I'm not occupying any moral high ground.' Her voice had risen fractionally and she took a deep breath.

'*No importa.* It doesn't matter.'

'No. No, it doesn't. So…thank you for sparing me the paparazzi camping on the front lawn, although if the world is dying to know the details of your broken engagement, then I guess it's just a matter of time before it all comes out in the wash and the paparazzi get here. I can handle it. I'm very good at saying *no comment* and, believe me, I don't want my life disrupted any more than you do.'

'You misunderstand. Disruption is inevitable for both of us,' Gabriel drawled. 'However, it will be lessened by your being out of the country until after the story breaks and the fuss dies down.'

'Out of the country?'

'Out of the country.'

'You're going to shuffle us off to some remote place in the middle of nowhere, hide us away for an indefinite period of time…'

'Don't be ridiculous.' Gabriel stood up and Alex watched him in confusion. 'The casserole. I can smell it.'

Alex leapt to her feet with a little shriek of alarm, temporarily distracted by the prospect of eating the charred remains of chicken and peas.

'I'm not being ridiculous!' She reverted to his sweeping solution to the problem of unwelcome publicity as she dished out two plates of extremely well cooked chicken and rice.

'I'm not going to *shuffle* you off to any remote place. Frankly, I can't think of one woman who would be less amenable to being *shuffled off* anywhere than you.'

'Meaning what?'

'Meaning that you're like a Rottweiler off the leash.'

'That's a horrible thing to say.' She wondered how they had reached the point where insults were being traded back and forth like two combatants fighting in a ring. A belated sense of fair play made her realise that perhaps, and only a very small perhaps, she wasn't being quite as helpful as she could.

His life had been a lot more disrupted than hers and he *was* trying to deal with it without drama. A pack of reporters in front of her house, she reluctantly acknowledged, *would* be hellish. If he resented her sudden, disastrous reappearance in his life and all the chaos it had brought in its wake, then how much more was he resenting her now, when she stubbornly refused to listen to a word he had to say because she was just too busy shouting at him?

'But point taken,' she muttered, sliding her eyes to him and then just as quickly sliding them away again. She reacted against every single thing he said because he just seemed to rouse frightening, primitive feelings in her that made a non-sense of her normally phlegmatic, upbeat personality. Hadn't she coped with the fear when she'd discovered that she was pregnant and the loneliness of having her child without the support of the father around? Yes. So that surely pointed to an inner strength, even though one look at that darkly handsome face made her feel weak and panicky. But if he could be an adult about the situation, then she could as well.

'Finally. We're getting somewhere.' He pushed aside his empty plate and angled his long body back from the table so that he could cross his legs. 'My parents have yet to find out what's really happening. I have only told them about breaking off the engagement.'

'I bet they were overjoyed at that,' Alex mumbled with a sinking feeling. Just when their son was about to tie the knot with the perfect woman, along came a serpent in the garden of Eden to wreck the whole plan.

'They have accepted it. But I wanted to tell them about Luke face to face. Which is where you come in. I will arrange for us to have a little…holiday in Spain. We can break the news to them together and introduce them to their grandson. It will also allow me time to…get to know Luke. Undiluted time. As a bonus, we will be out of the country and away from media speculation.'

From a detached point of view, it certainly sounded like a brilliant idea. However, Alex felt far from detached when she considered the suffocating prospect of her and Luke spending *undiluted time* with Gabriel.

'What about your work?' she asked, drifting off with sickening ease into all sorts of scenarios that would prove a constant, unremitting threat to her mental health. Gabriel eating meals with them, lounging around a beach with a towel slung over his broad shoulders, laughing and relaxed and horribly, horribly disturbing. 'You have an empire to run!' she blurted out, fighting against the image of the old Lucio slotting neatly into this new Gabriel, thereby blurring the lines of hostility that were so useful.

'Needs must.' He shrugged, coolly polite as he detected the horror in her voice. 'Sacrifices must be made. I am prepared to make them.'

'Your parents will hate me!' She speared a piece of chicken with her fork and looked at it miserably. 'They must be so disappointed at how things turned out between you and Cristobel and, when they find out the reason why, they're going to have me hung, drawn and quartered.' Having never met his parents, she was already imagining them as older versions of Gabriel. Cold hearted, ambitious, fabulously wealthy and one hundred per cent approving of a marriage based on suitability. She didn't think that they would be falling over themselves to welcome a jeans-wearing foreigner from a humble background who had been silly enough to have a fling with their highly eligible son and get pregnant. She cast her mind around for a punishment that would befit such a crime and could come up with nothing.

Gabriel felt his lips twitch with sudden, unannounced amusement. She had always had a flair for the dramatic.

'Maybe you could face them on your own,' she carried on, her voice adopting a wheedling tone. 'Luke and I could stay somewhere…else and then they could come and visit. For a couple of hours to start with…'

He was already shaking his head before she could get to the end of her sentence and she threw him a baleful, sulky look from under her lashes.

'You're being unrealistic. And they won't have you hung, drawn and quartered. They're not barbarians. Naturally, they are deeply conventional people and they will find it odd that we have no intention of legalising our union for the sake of our child, but I'm sure I can bring them round to your point of view.'

'Right.' Alex was not in the least bit mollified by his reassurances.

'So, now that you have agreed to this small step, we have to discuss the practicalities. I will get my people to see about selling this place and you can refund any money you borrowed to your parents. You will have to hand in your notice at your job, but that will be a formality because you'll be leaving for Spain next week. Is your passport in order? Is Luke on it?'

Alex looked at him open-mouthed. She felt as though she had suddenly been tossed inside a washing machine which had been turned to the spin cycle.

'I can't sort all this stuff out in a matter of a few days!' she gasped at the first immediate difficulty staring her in the face.

'You don't need to.' Gabriel paused and looked away for a few seconds before returning his dark, brooding eyes to her face. 'You were on your own once. You won't be on your own again.'

His words, low, husky and uttered with driven intensity, brought a flush of colour to Alex's face. They also gave her an incredibly warm feeling somewhere deep inside her. She had carefully cultivated a spirit of independence, knowing that one small person depended on her, but to know that she was no longer on her own was a seductive thought.

'I…I will want to meet my son before we head off to Spain,' Gabriel said abruptly. It had only been a matter of a few days and he hadn't known whether keeping away had been a good thing or not. Should he have rushed to bond with Luke? No precedent had ever been set in his life for this sort of situation and he had found himself immobilised by indecision, finally falling back on a businesslike approach to the problem. Sort out the details first and then meet his son, get to know him. It was a thought that made him curiously nervous and Gabriel was not a man accustomed to nerves. He cleared his throat and helped himself to another glass of wine. 'Is there anything I should know?'

'Anything like what?' Alex enquired, mystified.

'Likes? Dislikes?' He had barely registered the boy when he had last seen him and had serious doubts about his ability to bond with the child, partly because he had been absent for such a long time and partly because children had never figured in his life at any level. They could have belonged to another species. He just didn't have a natural empathy with kids and he couldn't see how that was going to change now, whatever the circumstances. He had avoided dwelling on that, choosing instead to focus all of his attention on the nitty-gritty of calling off the wedding and getting his secretary to initiate the process of rearranging all of his forthcoming meetings. Now, however, lay the unknown territory of meeting his son. It was a terrain charged with unseen landmines. What if the kid hated him? What then?

'He likes all the usual things a four-year-old boy likes,' Alex said slowly. 'You know…'

'Well, actually, no. I don't.'

'Are you *nervous*?'

'Of course I'm not nervous!' Gabriel thought it right that he should dispel any such hint of weakness. 'He *must* be into certain things, though. Trains? Cars?' Or was he too young for things like that? Gabriel didn't know. He was an only child. There were no nieces or nephews clamouring for presents and interaction on birthdays and Christmas. He had friends and a couple of them had young children but they had always been safely out of sight whenever he had been around.

'He likes planes,' Alex told him. 'He has a collection of them.'

'Good. We already have something in common. I own two.'

'Which is something we have to talk about,' Alex told him, laying down her ground rules before she discovered that each and every one of them was being broken. 'I have tried to bring Luke up to be grateful and happy for small things. I don't want him growing up to be a spoiled brat. So don't think that you can swan in here and shower him with expensive stuff.'

Gabriel frowned. For a start, he didn't like being told what to do. He also didn't care for her questioning his parenting methods before he'd even met his son properly.

'Don't expect me to sit back and watch my own child live in poverty…'

'Of course I expect that you want to contribute financially to his well-being! I'm just saying…'

'You're just saying that you have a right to lay down whatever laws you want. For the past four years, you've had it your way. Now I'm here and things are going to change. I have offered you marriage. You turned that down. Fine. But the alternative will not be constant warfare. We will present a civil and united front to my parents. And when we return from Spain, you will move out of this house into something I deem suitable for my son.'

'What do you deem *suitable*?' Alex asked in genuine curiosity because a guy who owned a couple of planes probably had a very different idea of *suitable* to most other normal human beings.

'Somewhere close to me, for a start.' He held up one imperious hand, cutting her off before she could establish her protest vote. 'Remember, Alex. This was your choice. The twenty-first century option. An amicable relationship working together to do the best by our son. What we had is history. This is what we have now and you will not fight me on it.'

Except, *was* it history? When the sight of her body sparked something inside him and the curiosity to see what that body looked like now, having given birth to his child, was like a slow-burning fire?

For the moment, though, this was the road he would take. God knew, she thought he was a complete bastard and, that being the case, he would keep all inappropriate impulses under wraps. No problem there. Hadn't he perfected the art of self-control?

CHAPTER FIVE

ALEX settled into the comfortable seat on the plane and closed her eyes. She felt as though she was closing her eyes for the first time in three days because life, in the space of seventy-two hours, had become a crazy roller coaster ride.

Gabriel had taken charge with a ruthless efficiency that had given her very little time to think and even less time to argue. Had he thought that, given half a chance, she would have dug her heels in and refused to go along with his plans? In actual fact, she would have loved to because the thought of meeting his parents and being subjected to their certain disappointment and hostility was terrifying, but there were no grounds on which she could object. She had rejected his offer of marriage and had thereby somehow ended up removing her ability to contradict any further proposals without sounding uncooperative and selfish, two traits which were unacceptable when there was a child to consider.

So her house had now been valued and was in the hands of an estate agent for sale. Even though she had tried to insist on a rental.

'No can do.' He had shaken his head without any apparent remorse at flatly turning down that request. 'Rental carries the unacceptable whiff of lack of commitment. The minute you don't get your own way, you'd be back in your little terraced house and I would be back to square one, with my son living in a place of which I don't approve, and subjected to a traffic-laden drive every time I wanted to visit.'

Of course, that was a blazingly obvious piece of exaggeration but she just had to accept that Gabriel was never going to consider her modest little house as anywhere near what his son deserved. And any trip spent crawling on a busy London road for longer than twenty minutes would always constitute an arduous and unacceptable journey.

Alex had folded her arms and muttered under her breath and given him a look of open incredulity, all of which he had contrived to ignore.

But her hands had been tied. And it didn't seem to help that he was being the perfect gentleman. She had stood on her platform and spoken her piece about not wanting either of them to sacrifice themselves to a marriage made for all the wrong reasons, had asserted her independence, had scoffed at something as Victorian as marrying for the sake of a child and had proclaimed that they could be perfectly good parents, adult, civilised and connected only by their son. She had got what she had wanted. He had been adult, civilised and perfectly friendly. In a detached, polite way that she hated.

And then she hated herself for being silly.

It had all been exhausting.

The only positive had been Gabriel meeting Luke.

She reached out her hand with her eyes still closed and placed it gently over the chubby arm draped on the cushioned arm rest separating them.

Her mouth twitched. Gabriel might have conducted the technicalities with military precision, but it had been a different story with his son. Of course, she had sat Luke down and explained to him that Gabriel, the man he had glimpsed for a few seconds, was his father, wishing heartily that there were books on how to deal with conversations like that. But

Luke had accepted what she had told him with a little frown, then he had nodded slowly and proceeded to ask her about a toy he had seen on television which he had to have because his best friend had one. He was too young to fully understand the implications of what she had told him, although she was pretty sure that he would wise up soon enough.

So when Gabriel had appeared at the door and introduced himself by shaking Luke's hand, the child had hidden behind Alex and only peeped out when Gabriel had extended the set of toy planes which he had bought as an ice-breaker.

'I obeyed instructions,' he had said, looking at Alex. 'Nothing too expensive.'

They had all sat at the kitchen table and Gabriel had asked awkward questions while Luke messily wolfed down his plate of spaghetti bolognese and looked up now and again to answer something in childish detail.

Now, Luke was sleeping between them, his head drooping against her shoulder, while, on the other side of him, Gabriel frowned at something on his laptop.

Alex half opened her eyes and glanced surreptitiously at him from under her lashes. No amount of tough talking to herself could minimise the impact he had on her every time she set eyes on him. Five years on and he was still drop dead beautiful. He had discarded his jacket and now, as though aware of her staring at him, he snapped shut his computer and turned to her before she had the chance to close her eyes and feign sleep.

Gabriel looked down at the sleeping Luke and thought how easy it was when he didn't have to wear his paternal gear. He had foreseen difficulties in bonding and he had been right. Meeting his son formally for the first time had been an uncomfortable experience. The boy had hidden behind Alex, clearly terrified at the sudden intrusion in his life of a complete stranger. Today had not been much better. He had been

gratified to see Luke carrying the set of toy planes over which
he had agonised for a ridiculous length of time at Harrods,
but he had still looked at Gabriel with barely concealed suspicion and gripped his mother's hand as though terrified that
he might be left with the guy he had yet to refer to as *Dad*.

'This isn't going well, is it?' Gabriel asked abruptly and
Alex frowned and straightened in her seat.

'What isn't?'

Unaccustomed to dealing with failure on any level, Gabriel
looked away and said nothing.

'You're not used to young children,' Alex told him reas-
suringly. In his dealings with Luke, she could glimpse the
vulnerability that was so alien to his nature and she knew,
with some deep, inborn instinct, that recognising that vulnerability would be a mistake. 'He really likes the set of planes
you bought for him.'

'He was less impressed with the real thing.'

'Maybe he takes after me.' Alex looked around her at the
high level comfort afforded by a private jet. She could have
been sitting in a tasteful lounge with very helpful waiting staff
who seemed to appear on cue, without needing prompting of
any sort.

Gabriel relaxed a bit. He slid his eyes over her long jeans-
clad legs and the fitted striped jumper that would have been
a glaring fashion mistake on any other woman but seemed to
be just right on her. If he had picked a person out of a hat, he
could not have picked someone less like Cristobel. Physically
and intellectually, they barely seemed to come from the same
planet.

'Don't tell me you're not impressed to death,' Gabriel said
lazily, almost forgetting the whole friendship thing she had
encouraged. Under the jumper he could make out the jut of
her breasts and the usual host of lustful thoughts sprang out
of their loosely contained cages.

'I'm not!'

'Liar,' he said softly, with one of those killer smiles that made her break out in nervous goose bumps. 'I remember when I showed you that Ferrari all those years ago and told you that it belonged to a local celebrity. You were awe struck.'

'I was a kid!' Alex said loftily, trying and failing to drag her eyes away from his face. 'Did it belong to *you*, by the way?'

'Will you throw something at me if I tell you that it did?'

'Well, I'm not impressed with that sort of stuff now,' she said. She had a sudden image of them making love in the back of the red Ferrari, which *had* impressed her to death at the time. It would have been a disaster, of course. They were both way too tall to ever do anything serious in the back seat of a sports car, but that sleek BMW he now drove…

She went bright red and thanked all the saints that he couldn't read her mind.

Then she wondered whether his politeness was so horrible because she didn't feel polite around *him*. Did she secretly want him to still fancy her? Even though she knew that his taste in women ran to a completely different sort and probably always had? Even though he was the kind of guy she had repeatedly told herself over the years she would never again get involved with?

'And I hope you don't expect me to bow and scrape to your parents just because they're rich…'

'I expect you to be yourself.' Gabriel could sense her withdrawal. Just when the conversation relaxed between them, she would pull back and it enraged him because, whatever she thought of the man he was, she should open her eyes to the guy he had become, a guy who was willing to stick around for a son he had never known he had. Did it get more praiseworthy than that?

'How much longer before we land?'

'Very soon.'

Alex's stomach clenched. He had told her that his parents now knew everything. His plan to tell them face to face had been scuppered by his inability to get over to Spain in time and he could hardly show up with a ready-made family in tow and expect them not to jointly collapse from the shock. So Alex knew that she would be entering the lion's den with no defensive suit of armour. She only hoped that they would be charmed by their grandson, even if they loathed her on sight, although if they were as stiff as Gabriel then she could look forward to some heavy going.

And they would be out there for nearly four weeks!

Alex had been stunned when Gabriel had casually inserted that into the conversation as they'd boarded the plane to Madrid. Two weeks of possible hell with his parents and then a further two weeks criss-crossing Spain, where he apparently had a series of houses in various places. He needed to get to know his son and he intended to do it on his home turf. What could she say to that?

'They're not monsters,' he told her with a hint of impatience. 'You won't be eaten alive.'

Between them, Luke stirred and curled closer towards Alex. She saw Gabriel note that imperceptible shift away from him and for a few painful seconds her heart constricted. Before she could be sucked in by her emotions, however, she felt the plane begin to dip and circle and then Luke was flying his pretend plane in his hand and bombarding her with questions. Somehow considering himself eliminated from the magic circle, Gabriel stared frowningly through the window and watched as the land beneath them got closer and closer until the plane was bumping along the runway and then, at last, coming to a smooth halt in the airfield.

Between the cluster of other small planes, against which his gleaming black jet stood out like a sore thumb, he could see his parents' driver waiting behind the fence.

'Alonso has come to meet us—' he turned to Alex, who was looking uncertainly around her as if waiting for the captain's voice to come across the tannoy telling her that she could safely unclasp her seat belt and disembark '—so you can put your nerves on hold temporarily.'

'That's easy for you to say,' Alex mumbled, finally galvanising her body into action and turning her attention to Luke, who was busily occupying himself in her arms, making plane-like noises and pretending to give orders to an imaginary crew.

'My turn will come,' Gabriel said dryly. 'When I confront your family and get beaten to death by your brothers.' His fabulous dark eyes met hers and she gave him a reluctant smile.

'I can't imagine you being nervous.'

'Good,' he drawled, tipping her face up to his before she could begin leaving the plane. 'I like that.'

That was so typically Gabriel, even the Gabriel she used to know, that she laughed and he felt his breath catch in his throat. With driving intensity, he focused on her soft, full lips, her pearly white teeth and then the nervous way her fingers raked through her short hair as she tuned in to his wavelength. For a second, the rest of the world disappeared.

Alex's breath caught in her throat and, when he reached out to brush a strand of hair from her face, she inhaled sharply before turning away with a slight stumble. She was horrified to find that she hadn't wanted that sudden electric connection to end and if it had to end, she had wanted it to end with him kissing her. How could she have so completely forgotten the nerve-racking present in favour of a treacherous, erotic fantasy? Luke had stopped the random twirling of his toy plane and was now contorting his little body in her arms so that he could stare directly into her eyes.

Flushed with guilt, Alex dropped him to his feet as soon as they were on the tarmac and her polite chit-chat about the heat dried up as she saw him reach out and unconsciously slip his tiny hand in his father's.

Above his curly dark head, Gabriel's eyes met hers and there was a moment of wordless communication before she looked away.

The long black limo waiting for them rescued her from dwelling on her nerves as it was a source of boundless fascination for Luke in a way the plane had failed to excite him. While she grappled with the ever advancing and dreaded meeting with Gabriel's parents, he squirmed and investigated everything there was to investigate in the car, from the little drinks bar to the dark windows to the various high-tech gadgets, there to make life more comfortable for the average billionaire. In the process, he babbled a running commentary on nothing in particular, peppering random insights into some of the other children in his pre-school class with a hundred questions about what in the car did what and why.

'He seems highly intelligent,' Gabriel remarked, looking at Alex, and, for the first time since they had stepped into the limo, she gave him a genuinely warm smile.

'I think that's called parental bias.'

With a mere forty minutes left before they reached his parents' impressive mansion on the outskirts of the city, Gabriel determined to employ distraction tactics. There was no way that he wanted Alex to be on the defensive when she met his parents. It would be a sure fire way of ensuring that the two weeks spent with them was a crashing failure. He hadn't been able to gauge the level of his parents' disappointment with the abrupt change of wedding plans via a phone call but he was banking on severe. Nor had he been able to decipher the depth of their shock at what he had had to tell them a scant twenty-four hours previously but he was also betting on severe. To add a defensive and belligerent Alex into the mix could be a catastrophe.

So he maintained a light-hearted murmuring banter about Luke throughout the journey, making sure to fill any pauses with conversation and focusing so hard in his efforts that he was barely aware of the casual ease with which he scooped his son on to his lap and ruffled his silky dark hair.

Released from his own self-imposed inhibitions, he was communicating with his son without even being aware of it and Alex was surprised at the tightness in her chest as she witnessed that unconscious breaking of the ice. When she had been pregnant, and when she had first had Luke, she had daydreamed about what might have been had she and Gabriel—or Lucio, as she had thought of him back then—ended up together. She had fantasised about being a normal, happily married couple. In her fantasies, he had related to his son pretty much the way he was relating now, holding him on his lap with those big, strong hands and bending to smile distractedly at something his son said.

She was surprised when she next glanced out of the window to discover that they were no longer on the main road but navigating through a series of small side roads, on either side of which orchards stretched away into the distance. It couldn't have been further from the dreary listless grey weather they had left behind in London and, for the first time, Alex felt a little kick at thinking that perhaps it had been right, after all, to remove herself and Luke from their familiar territory. He had never had the chance to go abroad. It was occurring to her that this would be just one of the things that he would be able to enjoy, being the son of Gabriel Cruz.

Trips abroad, big houses, fancy cars…they had been the stuff of Gabriel's life, not that she had known that when they had met. Was it any wonder that he passionately wanted the same for his son?

'We're here.'

Alex blinked and gazed at the sprawling mansion looming into view at the end of the private avenue. A massive circular courtyard, elaborately landscaped at its centre, fanned out to impeccable lawns on either side. Whilst it bore no resemblance to the stately homes in England, it was much too big to be classified as a villa.

'Your parents live here…*on their own*?' Alex asked weakly.

'There's staff.'

'Right.'

Gabriel looked at her incredulous saucer eyes and was catapulted back to that heady teenage feeling of having successfully impressed a girl. It was a feeling he hadn't experienced for a very, very long time and it felt good.

Against him, Luke stirred out of the catnap he had fallen into with the ease of a child and Gabriel looked down at the flushed little face staring drowsily up at him, weirdly confused and surprised. His instinct was to return the child to his mother, but he resisted the impulse and was gratified when Luke showed no signs of wriggling away.

'I can see why you thought my place was a bit on the small side,' she whispered to cover her nerves as the driver moved around to open the door for her. On top of everything else, she felt horribly underdressed for the occasion. She had dressed casually as a protest vote, wanting to establish from the start that she was her own person and would not be bullied by anyone. She was regretting it.

'Will we be living here?' Luke asked Gabriel with keen interest.

'For a little while.' Gabriel smiled. 'But you'll be able to come and visit any time you want to.' He shot Alex a warning look, just in case she was about to protest. 'Your grandparents would love to have you whenever you want.'

'Nan and Gramp live in Ireland.'

'And your other grandparents live here.'

Luke accepted that simple fact with a slight nod.

Alex barely registered that because the impressive front door had opened on a beaming couple. The man was tall and, as she drew nearer, she recognised those classically austere features, and the woman, coming towards them now, was small and round and amazingly unlined.

'Didn't I tell you that they weren't monsters?' Gabriel murmured, taking her hand, a piece of moral support which Alex knew she should object to but for which she was inordinately grateful.

He was smiling as he bent to kiss his mother and something else clicked into place in her head. Gabriel loved his parents. His marriage proposal had been his way of trying to capture what they had and provide it for his own son. Of course, there was no love in the equation and so it would never have worked out, but Alex was beginning to understand his motivations.

'Antonio Cruz…it is a pleasure to meet you…' He was extending his hand and smiling, as was the woman, who had also moved forward to introduce herself in accented English, but their eyes were on their grandson and Luke was positively basking in the sudden attention, allowing himself to be lifted by his grandfather and shown to his grandmother like some amazing long lost treasure, although twisting round just to make sure that Alex was still in sight.

This was hardly the cold, condemnatory greeting she had expected.

She was ushered inside the house and, when she began to awkwardly explain how sorry she was that they had not met their grandson sooner, her apologies were waved aside amidst affirmations of delight that they were meeting him now. Every compliment was paid to Luke and, waiting in the grand drawing room, an anachronism against the opulent, traditional decor, was a shiny three-wheeled bicycle of the sort Alex had never seen before.

'It is their way of expressing their enthusiasm about meeting him,' Gabriel murmured softly to her. He was as surprised as she was at the warmth of their greetings and wondered whether there had been truth in his father's remarks that the cancellation of the wedding had not been the disaster he had anticipated for them both. 'Please refrain,' he continued in the same low breath, 'from giving a speech about the evils of money.'

'I wouldn't have dreamt of doing any such thing!'

'Good.'

While Gabriel moved to chat to his father, his mother, Maria, drew her to one side. 'We can watch Luke in the garden on his new bike,' she said, not seeming to mind that he had already climbed on it and was experimenting with their gleaming polished floor as a possible racetrack.

'You must be very proud of him,' the older woman confided as they followed him outside, leaving Gabriel with his father. 'Gabriel explained the situation.

'He told us that you were unable to contact him when you fell pregnant. Distressing though it is to know that I could have met my grandson when he was a baby, we are both pleased that we are meeting him now and that Gabriel will finally be happy. As a mother, you know that is all we wish for our children.'

Alex flushed and guiltily wondered how this charming woman would react if she knew that her son *finally being happy* was not really on the agenda.

'Cristobel was not the right one for Gabriel,' Maria confided, chuckling when Luke paused to flash her a crooked sidelong smile that made him resemble a mini Gabriel even more than he already did.

Alex said nothing. Maria had romantic delusions about her son. She would be stricken if she knew that what was right for Gabriel *was* a woman like Cristobel who ticked all the right boxes except for that big box labelled Love, which didn't interest him anyway.

'You, on the other hand. The very minute I saw you, my dear, *I knew*. A mother *knows these things*.'

'Knows *what* things?'

Completely lost, Alex turned to Maria with a perplexed frown but Gabriel and his father were emerging from the house and any explanation for that weird remark was lost as Alex was plied with questions about Luke, who had the look of a child suddenly let loose in a sweet shop.

'Now, you must be tired,' Maria announced once they were all inside.

Alex realised that she was. It had been a long, wearying few days and, with the horrifying hurdle of meeting his parents behind her, exhaustion slammed into her like a brick wall.

'Your bags have been taken up and, if it is all right with you, Antonio and I would enjoy so much settling our grandson.'

Alex looked down at Luke, who looked as bright eyed and bushy-tailed as any four-year-old boy who had slept off and on and was now brimming over with boundless energy and excitement in his new surroundings, even though it was already past his normal bedtime. It would take more than a handful of stories to send him to sleep but, whilst she hesitated, Gabriel stepped into the silence and assured his parents that Luke would love nothing better.

'We bought a few books…' Maria smiled down at the child and held her hand out. 'Made the room as special as we could in the small amount of time…I hope you do not mind…' A quick look at Alex, who shook her head and gave in to the warm feeling inside her of being accepted. More than accepted…*apparently welcomed with open arms.* Her mind drifted sleepily back to what the older woman had earlier said but she was literally too tired to analyse anything.

'Of course, he will be in the blue room next to you…'

'You're practically asleep on your feet,' Gabriel said, amused. He looked hesitantly down at his son, unsure whether the affection displayed earlier had been an anomaly, but, risking it, he stooped down to lift Luke up and was rewarded with a shy smile which was fairly thrilling. He grinned back and ventured a more robust sign of affection, throwing him up in the air and catching him as if he were as light as a feather. Alex watched, feeling vaguely left out when Luke gave a shriek of laughter and begged for a repeat performance. He had no experience of men. Alex had had no boyfriends since she and Gabriel had parted ways. There had been opportunities and she knew that some of them had ticked all the right boxes, but she had never felt inclined to take any of them up. Her life had been too busy, she reasoned to herself, with Luke and with just making ends meet and carving out an independent life for herself, for her to make space for the arduous business of getting to know a guy. Sometimes, underneath that robust reasoning, she'd thought that no man had ever come along who could hold a candle to the Lucio she had known then. But she didn't like thinking like that and it scared her to imagine that he was now back in her life, harnessed to her against his will, a nightmare living reminder of her foolish teenage dreams.

The little game with Luke ended as Gabriel gently set him down. For a few seconds Alex knew that she had been entirely forgotten in the aftermath of his boisterous few minutes of fun with his father. From the sidelines, Maria and Antonio were looking on with every semblance of enjoying the sight of Gabriel playing with his son and, when Maria caught her eye, the older woman's beam became even broader so that Alex couldn't resist smiling back, even though it was a little disconcerting to witness this much delayed bonding finally beginning to take place.

'And now up to bed, both of you!' Maria urged them up the magnificent staircase that forked in opposite directions at the top to accommodate the various wings of the grand house.

'I'm sure Gabriel would like to stay and catch up with you.' Alex shot him a telling glance which she hoped he would correctly interpret as *tell your parents the full story of our situation*.

'Time enough tomorrow,' Maria said comfortably. 'And this little man will be following very soon.'

'Since I've been good—' Luke directed this question to his new found grandparents, taking full advantage of a once in a lifetime opportunity but making sure that he wasn't actually looking at Alex when he did it '—am I allowed some ice cream?' He flashed them a winning smile. 'Or even some chocolate?' And then, finally realising that permission might be required from a higher source, he shot his mother a pleading look and she sighed resignedly.

'You're a horror,' she told him grinning. 'But first, come and have a look at your room and I'll be checking to make sure you're in it in an hour.'

Thoughts of a lovely warm bath gave her a renewed sense of energy as they all trooped up the stairs and turned left at the top. For the first time since she had arrived, she really paid attention to her surroundings. There was nothing restrained about the opulence of the massive house. Lush carpet was soft underfoot and numerous traditional paintings adorned the walls, conferring the impression that this was a house that had seen many generations of the same family. It was odd to think that Gabriel had lived here as a boy. Was that why it had been so tempting to string her along under a phoney name when the chance had presented itself? Had the novelty of being anonymous been as powerful for him because of his fabulous background as the lure of celebrity might have been for someone who had come from nothing?

If only he had had a crystal ball and had seen that for every act there was always a consequence. Maybe then he might have stuck to what he had always known.

She blinked with a start when Maria paused to push open the door to Luke's room and then, a few minutes later, the heavy wooden door that was next in line.

It was a vast room dominated by a four-poster bed, not the modern, undressed, minimalist version, but a four-poster bed of the old-fashioned variety that was only ever glimpsed nowadays in magazines or seen in period movies. It was spectacular enough to produce a gasp from Alex, as were the rest of the furnishings. The large, ornate dressing table, the rich royal-blue of the floor to ceiling curtains, the wardrobe with its panel of exquisitely fashioned glass, which was reflecting their images back at them as they stood in the doorway.

'I have put you here…Gabriel's room is in the other wing and I know you would have wanted to be close to your son in the room next door…'

Maria's words echoed around her head and then crystallised slowly but surely as Alex's wandering gaze finally alighted on the clutch of suitcases tucked neatly away in the corner of the bedroom. Hers, Luke's…and Gabriel's. Louis Vuitton rubbing shoulders with cheap and synthetic department store.

She looked round in confused horror, trying to meet Gabriel's eye, but he was busy talking to his father while Luke hopped from one foot to the other, bored with the house tour and eager to get to the kitchen for whatever untold delights awaited him.

'Um…' Alex cleared her throat. 'I don't think this is quite right…' she ventured hesitantly into a sudden bemused silence. 'I can't help but notice…well…' She gestured to the offending pile of suitcases on the ground.

'We will take care of these,' Gabriel said smoothly, inserting himself between Alex and his parents and Maria's puzzled face uncreased into a smile. Luke had slipped his hand into hers and was tugging.

'Look—' Alex gave it another shot, although she had to angle her body awkwardly just to avoid addressing his back '—there seems to be a misunderstanding here…'

Tall though she was, he was, however, taller and broader and she was forced to watch helplessly as the troops departed and she was left standing in the room with Gabriel, who slowly closed the door behind him and turned to face her.

'I thought that went well. Better than expected, in actual fact.' He strolled towards the window and glanced outside before turning to perch against the broad window ledge, on which were arranged a pair of solid black marble sculptures of galloping horses.

'What's going on?' Alex demanded, folding her arms, refusing to be drawn into polite chit-chat and infuriated by his attitude of casual indolence when she was itching for answers.

'I don't get you.'

'Oh, don't pretend you don't know what I'm talking about, Gabriel!' Alex resorted to an explosive outburst and pointed at the stack of cases on the floor. 'Why has your bag been put in the room I'm supposed to be sleeping in?'

'Because this isn't *your* room; it's *our* room. And I am as surprised as you are. I wouldn't have thought that my parents were quite so liberal minded. Then again, today has been full of surprises.'

Alex looked at him in seething silence. 'I'm not sharing a room with you,' she said through angrily gritted teeth.

'You haven't got a choice.' Gabriel spoke with utmost politeness. When she bent down to reach for her two nylon suitcases, he was at her side before she could straighten and this time there was an implacability on his face that sent shivers down her spine. As did his proximity. As did the intimacy of their situation, with that hulking great bed behind her, significant and shockingly evocative.

'What do you mean? Of course I have a choice! Luke's room is big enough to hold a small party! It'd be no problem if I slept with him tonight until this misunderstanding is sorted out!'

'Didn't I mention to you that my parents are ultra-traditional?' His voice was like dark chocolate swirling around her, suffocating her ability to think on her feet. 'They haven't considered the possibility that there is no relationship between us.'

'But didn't you tell them…?'

'Tell them what? That you are happy for Luke to remain illegitimate? So that you can *do your own thing*? That they will only see their grandson when visiting rights are allowed? That he will be the innocent victim of an unstable background? Surprise, surprise. I thought that delicate matter should be addressed to their faces and by both of us. In the meantime, they have reached their own conclusions.' He spread his hands wide. 'Shall we interrupt their enjoyment with Luke so that we can break the news to them that they're still in the Dark Ages and that single parent families are the done thing?'

'That's not fair!'

'Right now, it's all we've got. We can think of a way ahead in the morning. In the meantime, it's been a long few days and I am not inclined to stand here arguing with you. The bed's big enough for the two of us. And now I'm going to take a shower. I suggest you get down to the business of unpacking…'

CHAPTER SIX

GABRIEL took his time in the shower. Alex wouldn't be going anywhere. Firstly, she didn't know the layout of the house and, secondly, she would never want to risk the deluge of questions that would be raised should she be discovered bunkering down next to Luke in the room next door. She had expected the worst and, having been showered with warmth, she wouldn't want to risk destroying it all by creating a scene. At least not tonight. Tomorrow was another day and he would cross whatever bridges required crossing when they appeared.

Right now, he would give her time to calm down because she had been ready to explode. In the shower, he grinned to himself. Women tiptoed around him, always desperate to get on his good side. Alex did the opposite. He wondered how it was that although she was the least girly girl he had ever met, she was also one of the most maddeningly feminine.

He felt revived after his shower and utterly relaxed, despite the disruption to his highly well organised and well oiled everyday life. He had left his computer downstairs and he decided to forgo the joys of being on constant call in favour of whatever the evening had in store for him.

Which appeared to be nothing when he finally emerged from the steamy bathroom with only a towel round his waist. The bedroom was conspicuously empty, although a quick check told him that the suitcases were all still intact.

Without bothering to go through the hassle of trying to find something suitable to wear to bed, Gabriel headed for Luke's bedroom and, sure enough, there she was, sitting on the side of Luke's bed and in the process of finishing a story in a low, soothing voice to a child who was fast asleep.

'The sleep of the innocent,' he murmured and Alex gave a little squeak of surprise because she hadn't heard him coming in.

And little wonder why! She looked down at his bare feet and her heart skipped a beat. She had come to check on Luke, make sure that he had brushed his teeth because there was no way that she intended to wait in the bedroom for Gabriel to emerge from his shower. She hadn't banked on him following her through to Luke's bedroom, least of all with…

Her eyes travelled upwards and she released a little sigh of relief at the sight of the fluffy towel wrapped round his waist.

'Couldn't you have got dressed?' she snapped, rising to her feet and depositing the book on the little bedside table.

Maria hadn't quite been telling the truth when she had said that they had done what they could to Luke's room, given the short notice of his arrival. The bed was in the shape of a racing car and every picture book imaginable had been provided on a bookcase that was cleverly designed in the format of a cartoon character. A giant faux fur beanbag rested in one corner of the room, right alongside an electric racetrack, complete with miniature sports cars and remote controls. Lord only knew how they had managed to kit out a child's bedroom to such an exquisite standard in the space of a couple of days but that, Alex assumed, was how money talked.

It was spoiling taken to extremes but she didn't have the heart to tell them off because they were so conspicuously thrilled to have a grandson, even one they hadn't planned on.

They had been gracious and charming and at great pains to conceal the bitter disappointment they must surely be feeling and for that she was grateful.

'I wondered where you were.' Gabriel lounged against the door frame, beautiful, indolent and off-putting, and waited for her to join him. 'I thought for a minute that you might have scuttled off to some far-flung corner of the house but then I spotted the cases on the floor and figured you had come here.'

Alex brushed past him and shut the door quietly behind her. The temptation to feast her eyes on that magnificent body was making her feel a little weak but she was heart-stoppingly aware of him as he fell into step alongside her and even more heart-stoppingly aware of their bedroom door closing behind them.

The room was big. In fact, vast by any standard. But not so vast that she could possibly direct her eyes to a safe spot. She reluctantly turned around and looked at him and her skin tingled and her pulses raced and she had to fight down the inappropriate desire to swoon. She wished he would just put something on but there was no way that she was going to repeat that simple request for fear of him jumping to the conclusion that she was affected by the sight of him. Which he would, in a heartbeat. Gabriel was anything but dim when it came to reading female responses.

Then another thought struck her. Did he even *possess* pyjamas? He never had when she had known him. Of course she had loved nothing more than that, back in those heady times, but, in their current situation, she could think of nothing worse for her peace of mind.

'You're staring,' Gabriel drawled. 'Should I feel flattered?'

Alex bristled. His behaviour had been exemplary over the past few days. She had demanded a businesslike approach to their situation and he had obliged. But this was his home turf and she suddenly felt very vulnerable.

'I hope you brought something…*decent*…with you…'

'Something decent?' Gabriel's brows knitted together in a perplexed frown. 'What does that mean?'

'Pyjamas. Long johns. Something of that nature.'

'Why would I have done that? It's not as though I was actually expecting my parents to put us in the same room.'

'Which they wouldn't have done if you had had the common sense to explain the situation to them.'

'Old ground, Alex. We've been put in the same bedroom. Get over it.'

'Fine!' She folded her arms and glared at him belligerently. The naked torso was really getting under her skin. As was the way he was deliberately making no effort to conceal it. 'But, just so that you understand the ground rules, I didn't have to come here and sharing a room with you wasn't my choice! I have no option but…but…'

'But I'm to keep my wandering hands to myself. Is that it?' Gabriel asked in a cool, amused voice. He strolled very slowly towards her and felt her exerting every ounce of will-power in her body not to cringe back. Cringe back *in what*?… he wondered. Fear? Repulsion? Did she think that he was going to do something to her against her will? He had had the foundations of his entire world thrown into chaos and yet he had risen to the occasion and done his utmost to make life easy for her. And his thanks? *This*.

Her silence confirmed her mute agreement with his question.

'Let's get one thing straight, Alex. I am not in the habit of making a nuisance of myself as far as women are concerned.'

'I never said that…'

Gabriel held up one peremptory hand. 'What gives you the idea that you are so fantastically irresistible that I wouldn't be able to pass a few hours in the same bed as you without trying to make a pass?'

'Nothing,' Alex muttered, turning scarlet. 'I just thought I should put down some boundaries.'

'Have I given you any reason to think that I am not a man of honour?'

'No, but…'

'You presented me with a son years after the event. I did not question paternity. Nor did I threaten to take you to court to win custody. In fact, I did the opposite. I offered to legitimise our relationship for Luke's sake. You turned me down because you felt your own needs and desires overrule the well-being of our child. Fine. You want a detached, amicable relationship. I have granted your request. Moreover, I have done my very best to protect you from aggressive and unwanted paparazzi by bringing you both over here, where I can offer seclusion of the highest order until our news becomes tomorrow's fish and chips newspaper. My parents have not censured you. They have not asked questions. They, too, have accepted the fact of Luke's appearance with grace and dignity and have welcomed him to their hearts. And assuming, mistakenly, that this is more than just a simple business arrangement for us, they have overcome their own natural prudishness and stuck us in the same bedroom, thinking no doubt that they were doing us both a favour. And, bearing all that in mind, you have the cheek to stand there and treat me like a sex-starved teenager who can't wait to jump you.'

Alex felt as though she had been assaulted by a mental battering ram. His choice of words was contrived to demolish her defences. He had been nothing but reasonable, fair and frankly second to none, his little speech implied, and yet she persisted in treating him like a common criminal.

He had managed to take the wind out of her sails as effectively as a pin applied to a balloon, even silencing the little voice in her head that reminded her just what Gabriel was like. One hundred per cent red-blooded male with more than his fair share of an enthusiastic libido. But, hard on the heels of that little voice, came another, telling her that perhaps she was no longer the target for that enthusiastic libido.

Now she felt an utter fool. He was probably repelled at the thought of sharing a bed with her but had been big enough not to make a deal of it. He respected and loved his parents and wouldn't throw their good intentions back in their faces.

She opened her mouth to tell him that they should set the matter straight with his parents so that they didn't have to endure a full two weeks in the same room, but knew that he would see no point in doing any such thing. At least not when they were obviously in their honeymoon period of misguided delusions. After all, resisting her would prove no problem for him, so why bother with the fuss?

'What do your parents think…um…our relationship is?' Alex enquired tightly.

'Naturally, they imagine that their son would have done the honourable thing and offered marriage.'

'They *said* that?'

Gabriel gave an eloquent shrug of assent. Not in so many words, he thought to himself, but they had jumped to that conclusion. He was sure of it. They would not have conceived a situation of shared custody and visiting rights. How he disillusioned them of their fanciful notions remained to be seen.

'What on earth are we going to do about that?' Alex asked aloud and Gabriel frowned. It still angered him that she found it so outrageous that he had asked her to marry him. Five years ago she would have leapt at the idea.

'We are going to do nothing about it at the moment,' he told her baldly. 'They're old. They deserve one or two illusions, at least for the time being. So get your head around the shared bedroom scenario and rest assured that your body is safe as houses with me.'

'Okay.' Alex lowered her eyes because he was just too much in her face for comfort. 'I'm going to have a bath.' She hoped that by the time she finished he would be asleep, and preferably would have done the decent thing and removed himself to the sofa. It might be uncomfortable and his feet might have to dangle a bit over the side, but needs must.

Gabriel watched as she flounced off to the adjoining bathroom and he heard the meaningful click of the door being locked behind her.

She would take as long as she possibly could in there. Hours, if she could pull it off. Anything to avoid the darkened room and the intimate silence. But face both she would have to and, outraged as he was that she would think him loser enough to try it on when she was a reluctant recipient, he was still in a pleasantly contented frame of mind as he unpacked his suitcases, whistling as he went and then, eventually, chucking the towel over a chair and slipping under the duvet.

With true gentlemanly consideration, he switched off the overhead light so that when she finally emerged from a bath that could go down in the record books as the longest ever, she was obliged to feel her way to the bed.

Having not foreseen a scenario in which she would be forced to share a room with Gabriel, Alex had given absolutely no thought to her sleepwear or else she would have bought something suitably hideous. As it stood, she was in her normal garb of a pair of small shorts, which left an awful lot of leg exposed, and a vest.

But at least Gabriel appeared to be asleep. She slipped into the bed, huddling as far to the side as she could without falling off and when, after fifteen minutes of barely being able to breathe for fear of waking him, she was still wide awake, she discreetly got out, found her way to the cushions on the sofa and quietly began stacking them on the bed into an impromptu partition format.

Watching her from under his lashes, Gabriel wondered how long he should remain silent and motionless before he got rid of the ridiculous barrier between them.

No time, he thought, like the present.

Without warning, he heaved himself onto one elbow and, with his free hand, he casually tossed every single carefully arranged cushion on to the floor and focused his eyes on her appalled face. His eyes had long adjusted to the silvery darkness in the room and he had fully appreciated the spectacular view of her fumbling her way to the bed clad only in the briefest of nightwear imaginable. It was the sort of nightwear that would have sent a shudder of horror racing down Cristobel's spine. No lace, no ribbons, no silk. The sort of nightwear that he would have considered highly unsexy on any other woman on the face of the planet, but on her rangy, leggy body looked amazing. She might not have had the long swinging hair or the drop dead good looks, but there had always been something curiously appealing about her and his body reacted to that *something* with knee-jerking intensity.

'Forget it,' he drawled. 'I'm not having my space restricted by a pile of cushions.'

Having thought him to be safely ensconced in the land of nod, Alex could only stare at the beautiful angles of his face as he looked at her. The super-king-sized bed was suddenly reduced to the suffocating dimensions of a carrycot. He was propped on one elbow and the duvet left her in some doubt as to whether the towel had been replaced by anything suitable. Or anything at all, for that matter. She could spy the sleek, muscular curve where his waist dipped to his hip, even though her eyes were strenuously averted.

'Why aren't you asleep?' she snapped accusingly.

'Is this another of your crazy rules?'

'My rules are *not* crazy!' Which was more than she could say for her misbehaving body!

'Are you telling me that erecting a foot high barrier of cushions is the behaviour of a sane woman?'

'I just thought,' Alex replied grittily, 'that it would be helpful…'

'Why? I've told you I'm not going to ravish you. Besides, it's not as though we haven't shared a bed in the past.'

'That was different!'

Gabriel was finding that hard to concede, considering that his body was reacting in exactly the same way as it had done years ago.

'I want those cushions back!' Alex was almost weeping from sheer frustration.

'Okay.' Gabriel gave an elaborate sigh and began to slide out of the bed, which elicited just the response he had predicted. A high squeak of alarm as soon as she realised that he was completely naked.

'Forget it!'

'Sure?' He turned to look at her over his shoulder, his face a study in earnestness. She could have thrown her pillow at him. Instead, she made a low, inarticulate sound under her breath and he subsided back into the bed.

'It's stupid,' he said in a seductively unthreatening tone, 'to make such a big deal about this…' In the process of getting back under the covers, he had managed to gain a few inches closer to her. She smelled good. Clean and fresh and soapy. She never had liked perfume of any sort.

Alex looked at him suspiciously. It was hard to read the expression on his face because of the darkness but she didn't trust him an inch and she didn't want to. It was hitting her hard that she couldn't *afford* to trust him. Her anger and her wariness and her distrust were the only weapons she had against the power of his personality. If she abandoned those, where would she be? She shivered whenever he was around and the sound of his voice was enough to induce a maddening meltdown of her nervous system. At least when she was spitting fire, she was keeping him—and *herself*—at bay.

'And, while I'm about it…' He lowered his voice a couple of notches and reached out to idly play with her splayed fingers. Alex was barely aware of the gesture. She was mesmerised by the honeyed gentleness of his voice. The silvery moon was touching light fingers across his face and the shadows and angles heightened the beauty that had always had her in thrall. 'You're right.'

'I am? Right about what?' Her voice sounded pathetically feeble. And he was still doing that playing thing with her fingers although she pretended not to notice because she liked it. It was dangerous but she liked it.

'Maybe I should have told my parents the whole unvarnished truth. Told them what you want and that they would have no choice but to accept it, but I was…' for a minute, he almost used the word *weak* but that would have been going too far; *weak* was a word that could not possibly be associated with him and she would never have fallen for that '…concerned about their mental welfare. Coping with the wedding being called off and then plunged into what they might have considered an unbearably stressful situation…'

'Understood.'

'You have no idea how relieved I am to hear you say that…'

'You are?'

'Of course I am. I can't think of anything worse than fighting with you.'

Alex had no idea how he had managed to get so close to her. She felt the heat from his body and, when he shifted, the brush of his thigh against hers. Her head was telling her to briskly wind the conversation up but, instead, with a frightening recklessness, she angled her own leg and the shock of nudging him and knowing the extent of his arousal was like being hit with a power surge of live electricity.

Gabriel made no effort to move. Instead, he smiled and murmured ruefully, 'Just ignore me.' By which he meant *just ignore my unruly body and the fact that I'm unbelievably hot for you*. How likely was it that she was going to do that? When she had pressed herself closer to him? When she was staring at him with hot, dark eyes and those slightly parted lips that were begging to be thoroughly kissed?

The ice queen with her issues about their past and her high moral principles about their future was melting fast but Gabriel wasn't going to be the one to make the first move.

But he *did* wonder what he would do if she took him at his word, rolled over to her side and fell asleep. He had discovered a streak of stubbornness in her that had not been apparent the first time round, when she had been gloriously his for the taking.

The prospect of a cold shower was not pleasant.

'And, while I'm in the mood for wholesale contrition,' he continued in a voice that whispered over her like a caress, 'I think it's important to know that I would have stood by you had I known about the pregnancy…' Gabriel realised that he *would* have and they would have married and there would have been none of this ongoing nonsense about her asserting her independence and not wanting to sacrifice her life for the sake of their child. Five years ago, there was no way that she would have turned down an offer of marriage. He could remember her youthful, adoring enthusiasm for him as though it was yesterday.

'It would never have worked in a million years,' Alex mumbled, thrillingly tuned in to his proximity even though she was fully aware of the health hazard it presented. 'Look at Cristobel.'

'Cristobel?' Gabriel was beginning to wonder how he could ever have conceived of marrying Cristobel. She seemed like a distant figure belonging to a different and somehow irrelevant life. Still, he didn't care for her name cropping up in conversation.

'You would always have wanted someone who fitted the role.' Alex felt a stab of self-pity and her eyes blurred. 'I was your time out and you would have gone mad if you'd ended up stuck with me for the rest of your life.'

'You're being ridiculous. And don't put yourself down like that. That *time out*, as you call it…' this whole confidence exchanging thing was crazy…but still '…it felt good.'

'I'm just being truthful. But it's sweet of you to say it anyway…'

'*Sweet?* Since when have I ever been described as *sweet?*'

There was such genuine outrage in his voice that Alex's lips twitched and she eventually laughed.

'I would have wanted to have seen you growing inch by inch with my baby inside you,' Gabriel told her huskily. 'I would have wanted to have seen the changes in you…'

With that powerful admission, Alex felt that *danger* alert sign flashing frantically in her head go completely off the scales and she drew in a trembling breath.

'You wouldn't have liked them,' she whispered, assuming that if there was one thing certain to put him off, it would be the thought of her getting fatter and fatter by the day until she resembled a beached whale.

'Did your breasts get bigger?'

Alex stifled a choking gasp. She had edged her leg back but just a couple of centimetres and she knew that he would be hard as steel against her and the thought was an impossible turn on.

'We…you…shouldn't be saying stuff like that…'

'Why not? I wasn't there with you at the time. It's only natural that I would be curious about what I missed.'

He made it sound so reasonable but there was nothing reasonable about the way her body was on fire.

'So…' he prompted, enjoying the exquisite physical ache of his throbbing erection and his erotic fantasies of her ripe, pregnant body. 'Did they?'

'Of course they did,' Alex mumbled.

'I have an image in my head…'

Alex moaned softly and her eyelids fluttered.

'Did you say something?' Gabriel enquired in a concerned voice.

'It's time for us to get some sleep. This arrangement…it's just not going to work…'

Gabriel ignored that half-hearted protest. 'Not that your breasts aren't exquisite the size they are now. Small but beautifully formed.'

'Please don't…'

'Don't what…? Turn you on…? Because you *are* turned on, aren't you? I know I am…but I also know that I gave you my word that I wouldn't touch you and I'm a man of my word… So, if you want to be touched, then you just have to reach out…'

A flare of wicked, reckless craving rushed through her body like a tidal wave, obliterating everything in its destructive path. Common sense, reason, bitterness, resentment…all the things she had been holding on to caved in like a house of cards.

Well, why not? she thought with sudden, furious intensity. She hadn't been touched for such a long time. No one since Gabriel. She hadn't even been *attracted* to anyone since him. So what if she had one night of pleasure? It wasn't going to commit her to an ongoing relationship with him. Things would stand just as they had before! Except she might have got this terrible thing out of her system. In fact, she *would have got* this terrible thing, this awful attraction, out of her system and she would feel a lot more comfortable around him instead of acting like a cat on a hot tin roof every time he came within two metres of her.

'Just this one time…' she murmured slowly. 'Just tonight…'

'One night of wild passion…'

Alex released a long sigh of relief that they were of the same mind. She missed his grim smile as she obeyed him and reached out to splay her fingers across his flat, hard stomach. She could no longer contain the groan that escaped her lips or the way her hips jerked forward instinctively.

'I'm not rushing this…' Gabriel told her thickly, pulling her towards him and grinding provocatively against her so that she couldn't help but feel the abrasive rub of his hardness against the soft cotton of her loose pyjama shorts.

He heaved his big body up and then lowered his head, plundering her soft mouth with his lips, liking the way she moaned and sighed as he continued to kiss her. He had the crazy feeling that he had spent the past five years starved of significant sex which, he told himself, had to be a load of rubbish because he hadn't been short of beautiful women in the interim.

He curled his fingers into her short hair and tilted her head so that he could trace a hot trail along her slender neck with his mouth. He hadn't forgotten what she liked, what turned her on. She was sensitive behind her ear and just there, along her shoulder blades…

He smiled with satisfaction at her little whimpers of pleasure as he retraced that familiar territory.

'You feel exactly the same as they you…'

'You surely can't remember what I *felt like*,' Alex protested, her eyes fluttering open to stare at him with drowsy heat.

'You'd be surprised what I remember about you,' Gabriel told her truthfully. 'For instance, I seem to remember that you like me paying a lot of attention to your breasts…' He shot her a wolfish smile as she blushingly looked away. 'Believe me when I tell you it was never any hardship…' He pushed up her vest to expose her body and had to close his eyes briefly to control the shudder of rapturous pleasure that slammed into him.

Her breathing was rapid and shallow and her skin was dewy moist and flushed. The feel of her long body was silky smooth under his fingers. He wanted to turn the lights on so that he could stare at her and fill his eyes with the sight of her body. He didn't. He figured that that would be one sure-fire way of ruining the atmosphere and that was the very last thing he wanted to do.

'I think your breasts are a little bigger, actually.' He cupped them expertly and then rolled his thumbs over her swollen, tender nipples. 'I wonder if they taste the same…'

The verbal foreplay was driving Alex crazy. She moaned softly and felt wild and wanton as she arched upwards, inviting

him to satisfy his question. He had always made her feel wild
and wanton. He had taken her virginity and taught her how to
be proud of her passion. It was all coming back now and she
could indulge herself because it was going to be just for one
night. He had promised and somehow that had eradicated all
sense of wrongdoing.

'Would you like me to taste them…?' Gabriel circled one
pouting disc with his finger and smiled with hungry satisfaction when she ordered him to stop teasing her. 'But I *like*
teasing you and you haven't answered my question…'

'Yes! Please…'

She gasped with pleasure as his mouth found her nipple
and he sucked hard, tugging it into his mouth and caressing it
roughly with his tongue until she was squirming and writhing.
She was making up for years of celibacy but she didn't want
to hurry the pace. She didn't want it to be over. But the way
he was taking his time, moving from one thoroughly ravished
nipple to the other, was driving her out of her mind.
Did he know how much he was turning her on? She opened
her eyes and looked at him and a slow smile curled his beautiful mouth.

She ran her fingers lightly along his broad shoulders, like
a blind person tracing patterns of Braille, enjoying the feel of
his defined muscle.

He, in turn, parted her legs with one hand and, still looking down intently at her flushed, averted face, slowly slid his
finger to explore her ripe wetness, testimony to her arousal.
He watched her moan and toss under his exploratory touch,
as he rubbed her clitoris with the flat of his fingers and felt it
softly throb under his touch.

When her movements became more uncontrolled, he re-
gretfully cupped her firmly, bringing her down before she
could tip over the edge.

There was the whole night to play with, though…She badly wanted to touch him. He knew that. And she would. In due course.

Right now… He lowered his big body and his mouth replaced his fingers as he stroked that sensitive bud with his tongue, rasping it over and over and pinning her hand down when she would have tugged him away.

'No…Gabriel…*stop* or I won't be able to control myself…'

Gabriel looked up just long enough to say, 'I don't want you to, my darling. We're in no rush and I want you to climax beneath me…'

A shudder of uncontrolled pleasure, yearning and desire rammed into her heated body and she let herself go, her body taut and then quivering as she was rocked by an orgasm that seemed to last for ever.

Gabriel waited for her to surface and then he kissed her tenderly on her lips and stroked her cheek with one finger.

'You should have let me wait, Gabriel…'

'Like I said, sweetheart. Don't plan on getting much sleep tonight…'

And she didn't.

CHAPTER SEVEN

ALEX shifted on the low futon-style bed and opened her eyes slowly. In terms of perfection, this moment of waking, with the mosquito net fluttering in the fragrant breeze that wafted through the open louvred doors, had to be right up there.

Gabriel would be walking along the beach with Luke, looking for shells or interesting pieces of driftwood. It had become something of a morning ritual since they had arrived on the island seven days ago.

Or was it six? Or eight? It had been alarmingly easy to lose complete track of time once they had left his parents' home in the city and headed down to his secluded beach house that perched majestically above a cove where the water was as turquoise and as calm as anything she had ever seen in her life before. It was a setting that could have leapt straight out of the pages of a tourist brochure advertising exclusive homes. The house was open and modern, with a sprawling wooden veranda and bedrooms that opened on to the front lawns and overlooked spectacular views of the sea. To one side, the rectangular infinity pool was the perfect setting for their evening meals, light suppers prepared by one of the two housekeepers who kept everything in order when Gabriel wasn't around. Which, she gathered, was actually most of the year. Ana and Edna had also proved to be immensely popular with Luke and, for the first time in four and a half years, Alex had been able to do what many women with young children occasionally took for granted when they weren't having to cope on their own. She had been able to relax.

And Gabriel had aided and abetted that. From that very first night sharing that bed, he had chipped away at her defences with his humour, his obvious enthusiasm to win over his son after their shaky start. So she had vowed to stick to her guns and not repeat their lovemaking… He had allowed her. Until, on night three, she had cracked and gone back into his arms.

And since then she had been on a self-justifying bandwagon. She had been weak, yes, but didn't she deserve to snatch this time before grim reality back in England could take its toll? There would be no question of anything permanent in their relationship. In fact, Gabriel had said that himself, had told her that they were just getting closure. And if that had sent a shiver of bitter disappointment through her, she had quickly talked herself out of it because she was no longer the gullible kid she had once been. She had been a single mother for years. She had grown up and out of that obsessive, consuming love she had once felt for him. She was safe.

Now, she would happily argue with Gabriel if she didn't agree with what he said. No longer did she creep around behind him with lovesick puppy eyes, deliriously happy to say *how high*? whenever he said *jump*.

She wasn't sure what her parents, or her brothers, for that matter, would make of the situation. They knew that she was in Spain but their version of events had been severely edited. She had phoned and spoken to her mother a couple of times and had been vague in the face of direct questioning. Mostly, she had communicated with them by text and had been thankful for its deliberately short, uninformative format.

That awkward situation lying ahead was just something else that joined the other *something elses* waiting to be sorted out when the time came.

Stretching pleasurably, Alex slipped into a pair of shorts and a halter neck top which she had bought on one of the various shopping expeditions she had done whilst in the city.

Outside, the sun was already getting ready to unleash its full force and it was warm.

She took a minute to look round at her surroundings. Beautiful lawns, thickly planted with flowers of every bright hue, the glittering blue of the pool, the cool, airy luxury of the house behind her with its expansive wooden flooring. Every day, she felt the need to commit something new she had observed to memory, ready to be dusted down and examined at some future point in time when the reality of it had been lost.

She had even sneaked a few pictures on her mobile phone, although she knew that Gabriel would probably disapprove. He was passionate about his privacy. Which was why they were there in the first place.

She had only to walk for a few minutes before she spotted Luke and Gabriel on the beach, squatting by a rock pool, Gabriel's hand protectively resting on his son's stomach as Luke peered into the water.

The shadow she cast as she approached them alerted Gabriel to her presence and he looked up at her, shading his eyes with one hand.

His dark eyes gave her a leisurely once-over and he grinned as the colour crept into her cheeks. They had made love in more positions than he could remember and she *still* blushed whenever he looked at her!

'Nice,' he commented, while Luke frowned and poked his finger into the water, curious to see what the tiny fish in the rock pool would do.

Alex stooped down and made random conversation with her son while she waited for her heated blush to subside. But it was to no avail because back it came when Gabriel reached out to stroke the side of her arm with one finger.

'Today,' he said lazily, 'I'm taking you somewhere special.'

'I didn't think we could get anywhere more special than this.' In one quick flash her greedy eyes had taken in the khaki shorts, the loose T-shirt, his lean brown legs as he stooped to accommodate his son and she felt that familiar tingle in her breasts, the way her nipples tightened in expectation of being touched. The intensity and immediacy of her responses to him unsettled her but she had learned to deal with that by telling herself that she was just getting her fill of him while she could.

And it hadn't escaped her notice that all talk of marriage had fallen by the wayside, even though she knew that it was the path his parents expected, although the subject had not once been openly breached. They undoubtedly knew their son well enough to realise that he didn't take kindly to his boundaries being broached or perhaps they were giving him space to deal with the sudden developments in his life before trying to push him in another direction. Alex didn't know.

'Ana is going to have a special day with Luke…'

Luke's ears pricked up at the sound of that and he demanded to know what was in store for him. The sun had darkened him and he slung one thin brown arm around Gabriel's neck and looked at him with the same brown-eyed intensity that was so typically his fathers. More and more, when she looked at the pair of them, she was struck by the uncanny physical resemblances connecting them. Had Luke carried all those similar mannerisms, inherited from Gabriel, while he had still been in the womb?

While Gabriel told him about one of the local guys from the village, a personal friend and specialist kite maker who would be coming to teach him how to make his own kite, his every utterance was peppered with a deluge of excitable questions. Every so often Luke's eyes would flick over to Alex, silently looking to her for support, then back to his father. To the innocent outsider, they would, she thought, seem to be the perfect family unit, which just went to show how deceptive outward appearances could sometimes be.

'And now.' Gabriel drawled lazily as they strolled back towards the house, 'you and I are going to have a day out. I have a boat and you can't see it from here, but it's a twenty-five minute ride to an island. Just you, me and nature… Trust me, you'll never have seen anything like it before…'

Luke was soon happily out in the back garden, intently watching Marco as kite number one was meticulously constructed. It had taken some doing to arrange this day to themselves and Gabriel intended to make full use of it. He had brought all his energies to work on making himself an indispensable part of Alex's life, the challenge being that he did so without her even being aware of it. More than ever now, he knew that the unconventional relationship she advocated was not what he wanted. Having never felt any particular urge to procreate, he had now reached a point where the prospect of a ridiculous twenty-first century caring, sharing situation with the mother of his child and his son was unacceptable.

But he had known better than to voice his thoughts, instead allowing her to believe that the hotly passionate relationship in which they were now indulging was little more than a brief stroll down memory lane. She was clinging to the illusion that she wanted her independence but she would come to him. He knew it. Hadn't she come to him with her body? Crept over to where he had been pretending not to notice her presence and blissfully surrendered to something that was bigger and more powerful than she could control? The answer to that one was yes.

On all fronts, Gabriel was completely satisfied.

'Who is going to drive the boat?' she asked a little nervously. 'You know I'm not good with all that sailing stuff.'

They had headed back to the bedroom and she was busy rummaging through her drawers in search of a bikini. Where they were going, she wouldn't be needing one, but he let her rummage anyway, asking her to change in front of him.

'You know how much I enjoy that,' he said, his eyes caressing her as he lay on the bed and folded his hands behind his head.

'Incidentally, I am going to drive. I refuse to have my day of peace and solitude with you cluttered by the presence of a boatman. Take your top off *very slowly* and then come closer.'

'Don't give me orders on how to change into a swimsuit!' But Alex was laughing as she undid the little bow at the back of her neck and at her waist so that the flimsy halter top slid to the ground.

Gabriel's bitter dark chocolate eyes flared with naked appreciation and she sauntered over to him, hands on her hips, her full mouth curved into a smile of pleasure and satisfaction. Out of all the uncertainties in her life just now, the one thing she was very sure of was the power of their mutual attraction. Gabriel wanted her, he really *wanted* her, even if she wasn't a blonde bimbo with pneumatic breasts and big hair. He wanted her as much as she wanted him and, at least on that front, there was equality.

'Closer,' Gabriel growled, catching her hand and yanking her over so that she collapsed, laughing, on top of him. While she protested about getting dressed, heading off, leaving early because she wouldn't go unless he promised to drive the boat really, really slowly, he positioned her on top of him.

'I agree with everything you say. Keep talking.' He drew her down to the perfect level so that he could fasten his mouth around one breast and begin suckling on it as she supported herself in an arched position with the flat of her hands. The little shorts felt like an impossible barrier between them and she knew that she was getting wetter and wetter as he continued to lave her nipple with his tongue and mouth.

'Now, now…' he said, reluctantly pushing her away from him. 'You really must stop distracting me. If we don't get going…well…I'll probably have to drive the boat really, really fast and I know how much you'd hate that…'

The boat, when they eventually made it there, was moored out of sight beyond the bend in the cove. Ana had prepared an elaborate picnic for them and Luke was so wrapped up in the business of trying to get a metre of tissue paper off the ground that he was barely aware of their departure.

The trip to the island was so beautiful and the weather so balmy that Alex forgot that being on the water induced seasickness. Or at least it had when she had been a child and had travelled to Normandy on a school trip in foul weather.

Also Gabriel was helpfully distracting her from the onset of any symptoms by insisting she see how to sail the boat and then making her recite all the technical terms, like a professor, so that they were at the island before she had time to think about herself and her queasy sea stomach.

And the island was beautiful.

'I used to come here often,' Gabriel confided. 'The house has been completely modernised and renovated but it belonged to the family and we used to take a lot of holidays there. I can remember sailing across to this gem of an island with my father when I was a boy.'

Alex could imagine him doing the same with Luke but she didn't say anything.

Out to impress, Gabriel gave her the full tour of the tiny island. The white sandy beach on which they had landed gave way to a thicket of trees and shrubbery but a path had been cut into the density and, in the heart of the island, a small, roughly fashioned cottage was the only sign of habitation.

Alex was impressed to death, as she had been with pretty much everything he had shown her over the few weeks they had been in Spain. Everything was testimony to a lifestyle which was ridiculously opulent and beggared belief.

'Do you like it?' he asked casually when they were finally back on the beach.

'It's beautiful, Gabriel. Everything I've seen since we came over here has been beautiful. Like out of a magazine. It's amazing to think that you grew up with all of this.' She now fully understood why he had been tempted to keep her in the dark about his fabulous legacy all those years ago. It must have been refreshing not to have dated a woman who knew exactly how much he was worth.

'Of course—' he gave an elegant shrug and pulled off his T-shirt '—my parents come from a different generation and a different place. Now, it would be madness to encourage Luke to think that all of this gives him a right to be lazy.'

'Even though *you* obviously didn't let it go to your head?'

'I'll take that as a compliment—' he grinned at her and patted the space next to him on the towel, which he had spread on the sand under overhanging branches that reached out towards the sea '—considering you've told me a million times that I'm the most arrogant guy you've ever met. Not your kind of man at all.' He waited for her to contradict the last part of his statement and was disproportionately irritated when she failed to take the bait.

'You work hard.' Alex approved of what he had said. She, too, didn't want Luke to end up a spoiled brat. 'Maybe that's what I should have said.'

Gabriel hid his frown. 'Of course, however down-to-earth we strive to be with him, he will always be able to enjoy considerable comfort… Frankly, I would like to bring him over to Spain as much as possible. Not just for the sake of my parents, who would be more than happy to travel to London to see him, but I find it extraordinarily relaxing to be in his company. It strikes me that I may have forgotten some of the simpler pleasures in life.' He wondered whether he should press his point by insinuating that she, too, could enjoy such trips with them. He had tactfully avoided all mention of the future lying inevitably around the corner but perhaps his diplomacy had been misguided. For the very first time, he felt suddenly unsure of success. They made the perfect lovers and she was as obliging as he could ever have hoped for the minute she fell into his arms, but was it only lust that motivated her?

Gabriel uneasily did a quick mental comparison of the woman he had now and the girl he had once possessed. The sex was as good…better even, if that were possible, but there the similarities ended. She was relaxed with him but no longer was she a slave to his every demand. Did he like that? Gabriel wasn't sure. Given their situation, it would have been a lot easier if she had just surrendered to his superior logic.

'I didn't think you liked those simple pleasures.' Alex sat down, clasped her arms around her knees and tilted her head to the sun, closing her eyes and enjoying the feeling of warmth on her face.

'I liked them five years ago…'

Alex stilled. She had to fight against the temptation to be encouraged into thinking that the man lying on the towel, inches away from her, was the same man she had innocently gone out with, believing him to be a carefree wanderer with great looks and an uncomplicated personality. He wasn't. That guy was a myth. The real Gabriel snapped his fingers and watched while the rest of the world saluted and jumped to his orders.

'The simple things in life are always the best,' she said non-committally, which was not what Gabriel wanted to hear.

'Are you going to follow up that statement with the cliché about the best things in life also being free?'

Alex glanced down at him. His proximity was having its usual effect of scrambling her brains. She could hear the cool, jarring note in his voice and she was assailed by an intense desire to avoid arguing with him at all costs. The past three weeks had been a glorious ceasefire and she didn't want to resume hostilities.

'No. I've really enjoyed my time here and none of it was for free.'

'Some of it was.' Gabriel's voice dropped a level and he pushed himself up to drop a kiss on her shoulder. 'You smell of the sun, *cara*.' He licked her shoulder, a quick, delicate flick of his tongue, and had her twisting round to face him.

Making love on the beach was something they hadn't done. With Luke ever present and knowing that the two retainers at the house, along with the other incidental staff, were always liable to be somewhere in the vicinity, they had restricted themselves to the bedroom. Now, the prospect of making love with the sun on their bodies and the gentle rhythmic sound of the sea as background music was like a shot of adrenaline to Alex. When he carefully pulled down the strap of her bikini, she helped him along by unclasping it at the back, then she placed her hand on him, feeling his arousal and loving the way it throbbed at her touch.

A consummate lover, he had always been the one to insist on satisfying. This time, it was her turn to be in charge. If she had had some of her scarves and a couple of handy posts sticking out of the ground, she would have tied him down, but instead she was obliged to order him not to move.

'I'm not usually the one taking orders,' Gabriel said with a sharp sense of anticipation, 'but I'm willing to give it a go this time…'

It turned out to be easier said than done as he was forced to watch her do a leisurely, provocative striptease. There wasn't much to remove but off came her top with agonising slowness and, by the time she was wriggling seductively out of her bikini bottoms, he was on the verge of losing control.

He had to close his eyes a couple of times because she was just such a turn on. Long rangy body, high breasts, no evidence of the baby she had borne years ago, although there were times when he had caught himself fantasising about how she might have looked as her belly grew with his baby inside her. No way was he going to add that further fantasy to the stockpile right now.

She offered every part of her body to his hungry mouth, allowing him to feast for a while before pulling back until he had to stop following orders and take her with a deep, possessive hunger that left them both spent and perspiring.

Between uninhibited lovemaking, and another session during which *she* was obliged to keep still while he tormented her with every sensuous touch imaginable, and their frequent trips to the sea, which was gloriously calm and warm, the exquisite picnic lunch was almost an anticlimax.

'Enjoy yourself today?' Gabriel asked, watching as she daintily nibbled at one of the sandwiches. He didn't think that she was aware of what a splendid sight she made. Having rubbed her entire body with sunblock, taking his time over certain parts, which had reduced her to a quivering wreck, he had forbidden her to put her bikini on again so he could fully appreciate every bit of her body as she sat, cross-legged, watching him with the same hunger as he was watching her.

'No. It's been hateful!' She laughed and fed him some of her sandwich and then shivered as he took her finger into his mouth and sucked it thoroughly, his fabulous eyes never leaving her face.

'One more night and then work beckons,' he said, which was like a bucket of cold water being poured over her and she looked at him with consternation.

'But…I thought we had a few days left…'

'You and Luke have. Unfortunately, I received an email last night; there's something of a crisis in one of my deals. I have no choice, my darling.'

'So this whole *thing* was my equivalent of the last supper!' She stood up and turned her back to him so that she could stick her clothes back on. She knew that she was being ridiculous. This *interlude* was not going to last for ever. She had known that all along. They had fallen back into bed because the lust was still there, hard and strong, but no amount of lust could change the reality of what was waiting for them back in England.

And she couldn't let it. Because…because…

A tide of mortifying emotion swept to her face as she contemplated the pass to which she had come. Sleeping with the guy she had sworn to keep at a distance ever since he had returned to her life. The same guy who had used her and dumped her years ago had managed to infiltrate her system all over again. She had foolishly imagined that time had immunised her against his devastating personality. How wrong she had been! He had showered her with his undivided attention and single-minded sexual assault and she had fallen like a house of cards in a high wind.

And now she was in love with him all over again.

Released from the box in which she had desperately tried to shove it, the unvarnished truth rose up to stare her in the face. She couldn't even use the excuse that he had pursued her because he hadn't. No, he had waited and she had gone to him. Had he planned it that way or had that been just a pleasant train of events which he had seen no point in derailing?

'Sit back down. You're being ridiculous. Overreacting.'

'Why didn't you tell me that you were going to be leaving tomorrow?'

'Does it matter? I would have brought you here anyway.' Gabriel stood up and put on his clothes.

'Why?'

'*Why?* What kind of a question is *that*?' Gabriel was finding it difficult to understand where she was coming from. From his point of view, his behaviour from day one had been impeccable. And now, out of nowhere, she was throwing a hissy fit over nothing in particular. Hissy fits were normally the equivalent of death warrants as far as women were concerned, but of course he was in a place where his options were limited.

'One last day of lust and passion before reality kicks in.'

'Is that what you think?' Gabriel spotted the chink in her reasoning before she had time to withdraw her impulsive remark. 'That I'm going to get back to London and put what we have behind us?' He walked up to her and tilted her adorable, suspicious face to his.

'It's what we agreed.' Confusingly, Alex couldn't quite remember the precise details of this agreement. They had been eroded by his stealthy, subtle attack.

'Since when do we have to stick to an agreement that was made before we found out that what we had forgotten about each other wasn't worth remembering?' He kissed her tenderly on her full, sulky mouth and felt her instant response. No matter that her head was shrieking at her to resist. Her body was obeying its own rules and he liked that.

Having not quite worked out how he would set about getting what he wanted, the opportunity now presented itself to him and since when had he ever been the kind of man to ignore a perfectly good opportunity?

He gave her time to breathlessly surface for air and then ran his hand along her side, down to her thighs, lingering on her inner thigh with delicate teasing fingers.

'Stop it, Gabriel.'

'You know you don't want me to… You *like* me touching you…your mouth…your breasts…you like it when I get between your legs and taste your arousal…'

'You're not playing fair!' Was that her voice? It sounded more of a low, husky, uncontrolled moan.

'I don't like playing fair. I like getting what I want. And what I want is *you*.'

He teased her a little more, letting his long, exploratory fingers drift across her stomach and circle her belly button, then he turned away so that he could start re-packing the picnic things, indiscriminately tipping them into the generous-sized basket before covering the lot with one of the linen tea cloths and heading, with his towel, to the boat.

'Come on.' He glanced over his shoulder to where she was standing, staring at him with a small frown. 'We should get going, Alex. It'll be dark very soon and when it gets dark on the water, it gets pretty disorienting.'

Giving her time to think about what he had just said, he helped her into the boat and got the motor going, sitting down to steer it away from the island.

'I've never seen a sunset to compare with the ones you find here,' Gabriel mused, thinking that he hadn't exactly been sitting around looking at sunsets any time in the recent past. 'I'd quite like to carry on sharing the experience with you.'

The lights of his house glittered like tiny stars in the distance as the glowing orange sun began its steady descent.

'I don't see how that's going to be possible.' Alex saw exactly how he might imagine that it would be possible.

'Don't you?' He swerved the boat towards the mooring on the island. 'I asked you once to marry me and I'm asking you again. This time I think you'll find my reasons more persuasive. Okay, I will concede that you may have had doubts the first time I asked, but we have spent time together now and you have to agree that we've been getting on famously.'

Alex saw the white of his teeth as he grinned, looking away from her and out towards the jetty by his house.

'That's just sex,' she mumbled and he shot her a look of censure.

'Don't denigrate what we have, Alex. You satisfy me and I'm pretty happy with that. Throw into the mix the fact that we have a child, a child who is now accustomed to having both his parents on tap, and what further reasons could you look for?'

Just love, Alex thought in confusion. That one little emotion that had not once been allowed to break through the surface of his lust. And wouldn't lust fade, anyway? Didn't it always? Unless there was something more fundamental to tether it down?

'How do you think Luke will feel if I disappear the second you return to England?'

'He's just a kid…'

'And kids are not entitled to be hurt? Upset? Confused?'

'I'm not saying *that*…'

'No? Then I don't understand what you're saying.' There was no way that Gabriel was going to let the sun go down on an argument. Not when he was stuck with having to return to London before the break of dawn the following morning. He spun her round to face him, his face hard and uncompromising.

'Let's get the facts down on the table,' he said, grimly steamrollering her objections before she could open her mouth to voice them. He also slowed the boat because a captive Alex would be infinitely easier to handle. 'I am a man of honour. I was prepared to marry you and you turned me down. I respected that. However, the situation has changed. You are now no longer just the mother of my child and someone I had a brief fling with years ago. We are lovers and I, for one, find that a very satisfying situation.' An understatement if ever there was one. She had managed to eclipse the memory of every other woman he had slept with, which was no mean feat. Considering she was now bound to him with bonds that were stronger than steel, that was nothing short of being an eminently desirable bonus. What if the years and the responsibility of single motherhood had turned her into a hag? Of course, he would still have proposed, but how much more tedious the situation would have been. As it stood, he was filled with a sense of well-being at how things had turned out.

'You can't deny that the past few weeks have been good. I've made substantial progress with my son and I don't relish the thought of having that come to an end and don't even think of giving me a patronising lecture on the richly rewarding relationship a father can have with his son with arranged visits twice a week with the occasional weekend thrown in. What we have is a good thing and marriage will make it better.

Stability for Luke and goodbye to all stress and strain for you. No longer will you have to do things on your own. This was meant to be.'

Alex was silent. She felt manoeuvred although every word he had spoken had been the truth. What they had had been good. Was there such a thing as *too good*? Because the fly in the ointment, for her, was that, like a fool, she had hurtled back into his arms and allowed him back into her heart. The sentiment was not reciprocated. For him, their rekindled sex life was proof positive that the traditional outcome he wanted was for the taking. By *meant to be*, he really was saying *the way I intended it to be*.

'Did you plan all this?' she asked in a small voice, willing back foolish tears.

Gabriel frowned. *Plan*, he considered, had never had a more inhumane sound and he didn't like that. He had lavished her with attention and had recaptured her sexy body with an enthusiasm that even he had not foreseen. He had made gigantic strides with Luke and had kept a watchful and protective eye on her when she had met his parents, sensitive to her insecurities. To try and imply that his consideration had been grounded in an ulterior motive was unacceptable.

'How could I plan that you would willingly come to me?' he questioned with silky assurance. 'How could I plan that the sex between us would be so hot?' He angrily raced the boat towards its mooring, slowing it into a sweeping curve only when the jetty was within spitting distance. 'I have done everything to please you and yet you treat my good intentions as a crime.'

'I don't mean to…'

Gabriel secured the boat with an expertise born of experience and grasped her hand to help her out. It was so dark now that she was little more than a shadowy figure but he could feel the very slight tremor in her slender arms and her quiver of hesitancy. It seemed very important that she didn't escape him and he didn't stop to analyse why this was.

'If we go our separate ways,' he told her in a driven undertone, 'consider the consequences.' As she fell into step beside him, he resolved to stop being Mr Nice Guy, waiting while she made her mind up. Only a fool played the waiting game indefinitely. He had given her the space she had needed. The time for politely standing back while she dithered and possibly made the wrong choices was over. 'Removing Luke from the situation for a minute, there's *us*…' he ground out. 'You can't sit on the fence for ever. That's not fair to Luke and it damn well isn't fair on *me*. It's make your mind up time, Alex.' He stopped and turned to her, wishing heartily that he could see her expressive face. 'I can't see you without wanting to take you to bed,' he admitted roughly. 'And I can't think of Luke without wanting to seal our relationship. But I won't wait for ever while you go through the pros and cons for the millionth time. If you don't want to legalise what we have, then I walk.'

'What do you mean *you walk*?' Alex felt the colour drain out of her face.

'I *mean*,' Gabriel asserted, 'I won't wait around for ever. Would you mind the thought of my bedding another woman? Getting serious about her? Do you want to see me arrive on your doorstep for my two hour stint with Luke with a woman on my arm?'

Alex felt as though the ground had suddenly been swept from under her feet. While she had been trying to sort herself out, she hadn't paused to consider that Gabriel might have been doing his own thinking. He was a man of action. He always had been. How could she imagine that he would have sat around twiddling his thumbs while she wrestled with her own fragile emotional state? The thought of another woman sharing his bed sickened her.

Gabriel responded to the lengthening silence with something close to panic. He could feel it surging through his system like poison, bringing him out in a sweat. It was like nothing he had ever felt before and he was rocked with relief when she said, with a catch in her voice, 'I…I don't like thinking of you with anyone else…'

Not even her afterthought, *'Let me think about it,'* could shake the rush of satisfaction that slammed into him. Didn't he always get what he wanted?

CHAPTER EIGHT

ALEX had the following day to really consider the development between them. Gabriel had left the island very early in the morning and she had wakened to a note on the pillow next to her telling her that he would be in touch later, to enjoy what remained of her stay, with a telling postscript that they would *discuss their situation* once she was back in London.

She had stared helplessly at that note, with its bold black writing, for a long time. Her determination to stick to her guns, to be a fully fledged twenty-first century woman who wouldn't barter her freedom for the sake of a mistake that happened years ago, seemed to have vanished in a puff of smoke. She was now having to face the fact that she had ditched all her good intentions for a man who might or might not have waged a deliberate war on her senses to get what he had wanted from the start, who had stripped her to the bare essentials and then offered her an ultimatum which he must have known she couldn't have refused. Did he know that she had fallen in love with him all over again? Probably. She had as good as admitted that when she had confessed to him that she didn't like the thought of him sharing a bed with another woman. The thought of that made her feel sick.

Not even the distraction of Luke and his endless excited kite-flying could distract her from the confused, hopeless train of her thoughts. So she married him because she was in love with him, because marriage would ensure stability for their son. Then what? She hadn't heard even the remotest admission from him that the union he wanted was anything more than a business arrangement at the end of the day, albeit one with the bonus of good sex. So what would happen when the good sex tapered off? Would she be left clinging to him? Hopeful that her love might spread to him like some sort of contagious virus?

By the end of the day she was exhausted from dashing around outside and was nursing a slight headache from her relentless analysing of everything. She wished that her brain had a switch, something she could conveniently turn off when it got too bothersome.

The house felt unbearably empty without Gabriel around and it depressed her to think how quickly she had become accustomed to his presence. She put Luke to bed and was further confronted with the reality of what Gabriel had told her because Luke was only marginally interested in having a story read to him. He was much more interested in trying to find out where Gabriel was and when he would be seeing him. She was beginning to realise that she and Luke were no longer a team of two. How would Luke react if Gabriel was no longer a constant in his life when they returned to England? He was only young now, but would he come to blame her in later years for depriving him of his father?

The magic of the island seemed to have disappeared now that Gabriel was no longer in the house and when she finally sat down to the simple crab salad which had been earlier prepared for her the food tasted like sawdust.

It was a relief when she heard the sound of the doorbell. For one glorious moment she wondered whether it was Gabriel. A cancelled meeting or, even more unbelievable, he was returning because he just couldn't be out of her company. That second thought she squashed with ruthless speed as she headed for the front door.

Both housekeepers had already left for the evening and far more likely it was one of them who had forgotten something. It was not that unusual an occurrence. They both had quarters at the house and Ana, particularly, was prone to forgetting some item of clothing or book or personal possession which she had left in her room.

But the interruption was a blessed relief from her thoughts and she was smiling as she pulled open the door halfway, looking forward to enticing whichever of the housekeepers it happened to be into some conversation. She had enjoyed practising her Spanish with both of them and was interested in their lives outside the splendid house.

In her head, there was no room for the unexpected and her shock at seeing Cristobel on her doorstep made her stumble backwards.

'You!'

'I know. I don't suppose you were expecting me.' She placed one hand on the door and Alex noticed that her nails were beautifully manicured and painted a vibrant shade of red. It was an insignificant detail but it distracted her momentarily from the nervous banging of her heart against her ribcage.

'What do you want?'

'To have a girlie chat, of course. What else?'

'I really don't think that Gabriel…'

'But Gabriel's not here, is he? He is in London.'

'How do you know that?'

'I don't *do* doorstep conversations.' Cristobel flashed her a cool smile and pushed against the door.

Of course Alex could have slammed the door in her face. She was, after all, a good six inches taller than the diminutive blonde. Taller, stronger but, unfortunately, she afterwards thought, lacking in the necessary aggression. Would Bambi have come out on top against a pit bull intent on destruction?

Okay, so she wasn't, an hour an a half later, having to apply plaster to open wounds, but her head was reeling.

She was surprised that she had managed to shove the thought of Gabriel's ex-fiancée to the back of her mind with such single-minded efficiency. She had no idea how she had been represented in the gossip columns. Newspapers had been non-existent for the past few weeks. She had cocooned herself in a bubble and, except for the occasional vague notion that *reality* was waiting *back home*, she had successfully managed to stifle anything too demanding.

Cristobel's appearance, she now thought, had brought all that up to the surface.

She had no idea where the other woman had gone after she had left the house and she didn't care. She had just wanted to be rid of the venomous blonde's presence, the blonde who had flicked her hair and looked at her with hard, bright eyes and told her that Gabriel had only hooked up with her through a misguided sense of duty, that his heart would always belong to *her*, that she would get him back and would have him in her bed just as soon as the whole *duty thing* wore off, because wear off it inevitably would.

'You may think that you've won,' she had said with a cool smile, while those diamond-hard eyes had given her the once-over and found her lacking in all the important departments, 'but you haven't. You haven't got the class or the looks to keep him and the fact that you haven't got an engagement ring on your finger is proof enough of that. A man like Gabriel might like tradition but playing happy families with a woman he doesn't give a damn about isn't his style. You might speak a little Spanish but you have a lot to learn about how a Spaniard thinks, especially a Spaniard like Gabriel.'

Replaying the conversation in her head, Alex groaned aloud and stuck buried her face in a pillow.

She wondered if it had been that final dig that had prompted her to say, with a calmness she hadn't imagined possible, 'Gabriel has already proposed. In fact, Gabriel has proposed more than once and, not that it's any of your business, we'll be getting married as soon as I return to England.' Well, it had been worth it to see that flash of anger that contorted Cristobel's beautiful face. She had almost been tempted to spin a fairy story about Gabriel being madly in love with her, but not even she could fashion a lie that was so outrageous.

Now, of course, she was left with the residue from that brief moment of retaliation but she began to wonder whether the thought of accepting his proposal hadn't been there, playing away at the back of her mind, since he had left, like the familiar strains of background music, just discernible but not jarring enough to require attention.

She rolled over onto her side, eyes wide open. With pernicious determination, she felt a little seed of hope bury itself inside her and take root.

Yes, she could think pessimistically about Gabriel's proposal. Yes, she could work herself up into a lather predicting worst case scenarios.

But she loved him and wasn't it possible that he might come to feel the same about her? He was attracted to her, there was no doubt about that, and if she continued to make herself exciting to him, then was it really inevitable that he would stray? Hadn't she read somewhere that men were creatures of habit? Or something like that?

She hurriedly closed her mind to the unlikely thought of Gabriel being a *creature of habit*.

In the morning, she would leave and head back to London with her mind made up.

Decision made, Alex found it difficult to sleep. Memories of Cristobel's attack on her were replaced by hungry curiosity as to how Gabriel would react to her acceptance of his proposal. Would he be relieved that he had finally won, got his own way? Or surprised that she had given up the fight at long last? Or would he be ecstatic and declare his undying love for her? That last improbable scenario kept her smiling for the remainder of the following day.

'I wish we weren't going back to London,' Luke complained as she tugged him through airport security. No private jet this time. She was leaving ahead of schedule so that she could surprise Gabriel and what kind of surprise would it be if she had to call him to sort out his jet?

'You'll be seeing your dad, though. Aren't you looking forward to that?'

Leading questions about Gabriel were always a sure fire way of captivating Luke's attention. He had developed an inexhaustible thirst to find out everything he could about his father, although this usually filtered down to awestruck eulogies about the guy who had already succeeded in filling the role of the strongest, fastest, cleverest dad, at least compared to the other dads he pulled out of the hat from his kindergarten class. Alex had met a couple of those particular dads in question and it was easy to understand why. How could the average man, hair thinning and stomach thickening, ever compare to Gabriel? The fact was that Gabriel towered above the average *human being*. He would always be the one outrunning the other dads in the fathers' race on sports days and grabbing the attention of every teacher at parents evenings.

Not too long ago, she would have found it impossible to associate Gabriel with stuff as tedious as school sports days and parents' evenings, but she had see him throw himself into the role of winning his son over. Whatever he did, he did with the full weight of his conviction. She guessed that would include everything that got thrown at him in terms of his duties as far as Luke was concerned.

Like the irrepressible force of a powerful undertow, this brought her thoughts right back to square one: how far would Gabriel go to complete the perfect husband role? He would move mountains for his son…but for *her*?

She would have to lay down one or two ground rules. Capitulation wouldn't be solely on his terms.

Arriving back in London was like suddenly finding herself flung head first into a prison cell from which she had temporarily been released. Even Luke appeared to have gone into a slump as he tightly clutched her hand through airport security. His interminable chatter had petered out to the occasional doleful and nostalgic remark about the beach or his precious kite, which he had been persuaded to leave behind due to lack of suitcase space, or the glorious big house belonging to his grandparents. Bracing talk about school the following Monday and his favourite, fish and chips, for dinner was greeted with lukewarm enthusiasm. Only the promise of phoning Gabriel met with a positive response, and since that was precisely what Alex was itching to do, she dialled Gabriel's number pretty much as soon as she had settled Luke in the sitting room with his favourite cartoon and a snack.

About to leave for a meeting, Gabriel recognised Alex's telephone number. Without skipping a beat, he told his secretary to cancel his meeting and, with experience born from long service, his secretary reached for her phone, also without skipping a beat.

Gabriel had been surprised to discover how much he enjoyed hearing her voice at the end of a line. He relaxed back into his leather chair and swivelled it round so that he was staring at the fairly boring panorama of grey sky, scudding clouds and tips of buildings.

'Am I interrupting you?'

'Wall to wall meetings,' Gabriel said, loosening his tie. 'But no big deal.' He wasn't going to be drawn into letting her think that she could do as she pleased. Work had always been the foundation of his life and, even if he had taken a break, a much needed break, for a short while, it was *still* the foundation of his life. It was what made him the success story he was today.

Women had never been allowed to overstep those boundaries and the fact that he had just cancelled his high level meeting for a phone call was testament to the fact that she occupied a special place. She was the mother of his son. He was quite pleased that, in a roundabout way, this seemed to elevate him to a flattering level.

'How is Luke? Is he missing me?' Then, before she could answer that, he continued in a roughened voice, 'Are *you* missing me? Would you be insulted if I told you that I had to take a very cold shower last night because I couldn't get you out of my head?'

How was it that the sound of his voice could do foolish things to her body? Her cheeks reddened and the telltale signs of that craving of hers spread through her body, leaving her damp and hot and flustered.

But she didn't intend to let that reduce her to a weak, stammering mess. She thought back to Cristobel and that hideous attack on her. Had she been telling the truth? Did Gabriel's heart really belong to the blonde? He had been drawn enough to her to propose marriage so that said *something*. And now here she was, on the brink of accepting his marriage proposal and, when she stripped away all the lust and sex, she was left with a business arrangement. Her return to London had been salutary in helping her remember that. As had Cristobel.

'I'm back in London, actually.'

Gabriel smiled slowly. Her return could only mean that she was lonely without him around and, despite the fact that he had never cared for the dependent, clingy type, he realised and accepted with stunning alacrity that Alex somehow didn't fall into this category.

'Where in London?'

'Where do you think, Gabriel? My house, of course.'

'We'll have to do something about that,' he murmured, half to himself.

'I'd like to talk to you, but not on the phone. Face to face. Would you be able to get away some time later this evening?'

'I can get away right now.'

'What about those wall to wall meetings?'

'You'd be surprised how flexible they could be.'

'No...' *Right now* seemed a little too sudden. 'I need to settle in for a bit. There's stuff to do around here.'

'Stuff to do? What stuff?' Gabriel frowned because *stuff* had never been offered up as an excuse not to see him by any woman.

'I need to get Luke changed and fed and I need to unpack and have a shower and wash my hair... Why don't you come around six-thirty? You can have some time with Luke and then we can...chat. I'll fix something to eat. Although I'm not sure what I've got in the fridge. Actually, I haven't got anything in the fridge. Maybe I could pop out and buy one or two things...'

'*I'll* bring something over!'

'You don't know what I need.'

'You need food. I'll bring food.'

'Okay.' She resisted the temptation to ask whether he knew where his local supermarket was and then concluded that he would probably send someone out to buy a few items on his behalf.

Would this be their life together? Extreme wealth and privilege that would inevitably remove Luke, and her, from the realms of the ordinary? Did she want that for her son? She realised that she didn't. She had had a richly, rewarding and very grounded upbringing and that was something she intended to confer upon her son.

'And I don't want to be fussy here,' she said, as gently as she could, predicting a blank wall of incomprehension that would greet her conditions, 'but Luke's had a pretty rich diet for the past few weeks. It would do him good to have simple home-cooked fare.'

'Okay. You're losing me here.' Gabriel raked his fingers through his hair and fought off a feeling of having suddenly been dumped in quicksand. He had no idea what she was talking about but, strangely enough, he would still have had the conversation, given the choice between that and his meeting. 'He's had the finest food money could buy in Spain. Pretty healthy too.' He frowned. 'I'm sure there was lots of fish.'

'Maybe you could just pick up some bread and butter and other essentials and some baked beans. Oh, and something simple for us to eat.'

'Simple like what?'

'I'll leave it up to you. Anyway, I think I hear Luke. I've left him in the sitting room watching a cartoon. He's missed that a bit, watching cartoons, I think… See you later.'

Gabriel gazed at the phone in stupefaction as he heard the distinctive sound of a disconnected line.

However, instead of fully appreciating the rest of his day and proceeding with the important business of running his empire, he managed to find himself wandering around a supermarket two hours later with a trolley and not much of an idea as to what to put in it.

At six-thirty, Alex opened the door to a dishevelled-looking Gabriel, still in his suit and holding three carrier bags with a couple more on the ground by his feet.

'I come complete with shopping. I can't overestimate that achievement, considering I had to battle with a trolley that seemed to have a mind of its own.' She looked fresh and clean and sexy-as-hell in a pair of old jogging bottoms and a T-shirt that barely skimmed her flat, tanned stomach.

'So I see. Come on in. Luke's been clamouring for you.'

She opened the door, feeling very ordinary next to him, and Luke bounded out behind her like an eager puppy hearing the sound of its master's footsteps. Several drawings were thrust at Gabriel, who looked at them with a gravity that thrilled Luke to death and made Alex smile because representational art was not exactly Luke's forte. Objects were pointed out with engaging earnestness and all adult conversation was lost in the deluge of excitable childish chatter.

'You bought the baked beans.' She held up a four pack and turned it around with an expression of mock wonder. 'I didn't think you'd remember.'

So it was baked beans on toast with cheese for Luke and only when he had finally been settled into bed did she and Gabriel reconvene in the kitchen.

Having felt calm and controlled amidst the chaos of having Luke around as the centre of attention, she was now very much aware of Gabriel's *presence*, that certain something he possessed that allowed him to own the space around him, and unfortunately her with it.

'You never answered my question…' His dark-as-night eyes roamed over her until she turned pink under the scrutiny.

'What question?'

'Did you miss me?'

Stupid question, Alex thought. *Did a fish miss water when it was removed from it?* He hadn't come any closer to her.

In fact, he had adopted a seat at the table while she remained standing, leaning against the kitchen counter, but she still felt as though she was being touched.

'Is sex all you think about?'

'It's definitely been on my mind pretty much since I returned to London.'

Alex wondered whether she should now be expected to simper with pleasure. She folded her arms and delivered a long, cool look which was like water off a duck's back, apparently, because Gabriel matched her look with an amused gleam in his eyes.

'Is the Ice Queen back in residence?'

'There's more to life than sex.'

'Really?' He threw her a wolfish grin. 'I wish you'd run those alternatives by me. I'm all ears.'

'For goodness' sake, Gabriel! You are *so* childish sometimes.'

'It's so refreshing being with a woman who feels free to criticise me,' he said with infuriating good humour. 'I didn't know what you wanted to eat, by the way, so I bought a variety of things.'

'So I saw.' She turned to glance at the improbable stack of items residing on her kitchen counter. Fresh tiger prawns and fillet steak nudged shoulders with lots of attractive jars and bottles containing interesting-sounding sauces whilst essentials such as eggs, milk and cheese had obviously not found favour, due to their lack of immediate sex appeal. She sighed. Even when it came to food, Gabriel would always make a beeline for whatever was easiest on the eye.

She began scrutinising the products and finally did the best she could with the prawns and whatever sauces seemed the least flamboyant.

'I've given a lot of thought to what you said about the benefits of getting married,' she said casually with her back to him, even though she could feel his eyes boring into her, making her clumsy with the knife.

'And…?' Gabriel found that he was holding his breath. Ridiculous.

'And I've decided that you're right.' *Keep it on a business level*, Alex reminded herself. *Use the language he understands.* She flicked on the stove, busying herself with heating the sauces, while her heart continued to pound like a jack hammer inside her.

Eventually, when she could no longer hide behind the business of stirring a sauce and watching a pot of pasta boil, she turned round to look at him.

God, why did he have to be so *beautiful*? He would object to that description, but he really was *beautiful* and that sheer overwhelming, masculine beauty made it doubly difficult to talk to him with the detachment she needed. She drew in a shaky breath and moved to sit opposite him.

'Good. I knew you would come to your senses sooner or later.'

'You've become an important part of Luke's life and it would be wrong to yank him away when he's become accustomed to you. In retrospect, it may have been a mistake to take that prolonged holiday in Spain. It might have been better for you to get to know him over here, on his own territory, where he could have maintained some kind of a distance…'

Gabriel's mouth tightened. 'Is it your mission,' he asked softly, 'to find things to say that enrage me?'

'Of course not!' And nor had she been fair. Didn't she *want* what was best for Luke? Those snatched weeks in Spain had been the happiest in her son's life. But somewhere inside her was the voice of self-protection telling her that she needed to make sure that Gabriel didn't think that he had scored a home run, that it was essential to maintain *some* distance between them, even if that distance was a front.

'I'm saying that I feel I've been put in the position where I haven't got much of a choice…'

'And I should feel better? Wrong choice of wording.'

'Sorry, but it's the truth.' She remembered Cristobel, the spurned ex-fiancée. She remembered his threats that he would find someone else if she walked away from him. Both were significant markers in indicating the direction she should choose to go and a complete cave-in wasn't on the signpost.

Gabriel raked his fingers through his hair and gave her a dark, fulminating look. 'I don't want to have an argument with you,' he told her with what he considered considerable self-restraint. 'You have made me very happy in agreeing to be my wife. We should be celebrating.' He stood up and fetched them both glasses. He had bought three bottles of wine. He opened the Chablis now and poured them both a glass, while she set the plates on the table in silence, thinking about phase two of what she needed to say.

'Okay,' Alex cleared her throat and gazed down at the food, which looked unappetising, despite the *no expense spared* approach to food shopping Gabriel had clearly taken. She sipped some of the wine, which was delicious. 'There are just a few ground rules I think we need to get straight before we go ahead with this…um…plan…'

Gabriel frowned. He didn't care for the word *plan*, even though he would have been the first to admit that marriage as a sensible merger had always been his way forward. He had become engaged to Cristobel because it had made sense at the time, and he had proposed to Alex because of the situation in which he had found himself. He was programmed into the ways of tradition. It would have been unthinkable to have continued his relationship with Cristobel, given the circumstances. On every front, he would readily have admitted that marrying Alex was the most logical, indeed inevitable, course of action. But, somehow, he didn't like to think that she was beginning to see it his way. It was a thought that confused him.

'*Ground rules?* What *ground rules*? We're not planning a military campaign.'

'I used to think that marriage was all about romance but now I realise that it's all about a sensible outcome. I realised that in Spain when I saw how happy Luke was, having both parents on tap. He's only young now, but that will become more and more important the older he gets. I never thought I'd agree with you when you first asked me to marry you because it made sense. I couldn't think of marriage to anyone in terms of a balance sheet but…' she shrugged and looked away '…you were right and I was wrong.'

Gabriel wondered how it was that being right sounded so pointless. Hadn't he got what he had wanted? Yes, he had! He focused on that and shook off his feelings of dissatisfaction.

This didn't seem to be the right conclusion to good news. Shouldn't they be making love right about now?

'What,' Alex asked with genuine curiosity, 'turned you off the concept of marrying for love? I mean, your parents are so happy and so in love with one another…'

'…That it should have washed off on me somehow?' Gabriel flushed darkly. He had always felt the weight of expectation on his shoulders. That he would fall madly in love, get married and live in perfect bliss with a litter of kids until the day he died. 'I left home at sixteen to board and then university here and, except for a few breaks in between…' one of them being the very break that had landed him in this situation '…I was destined to carry the weight of my father's legacy on my shoulders. At the time, it was going through some financial troubles. Appalling management in some of its branches.

Trouble with unions in other parts. I buried myself deep in my work. There was a lot to do and I was surrounded by other people who were similarly committed to long hours and one hundred per cent dedicated service to the various companies. You'd be surprised how many marriages fall by the wayside when there's no husband in evidence for little Johnny's prize-giving. You can say that that was more of a learning curve for me than my parents' blissful contentment.'

'That's terrible,' Alex murmured, truly shocked. 'What's the point in working twenty-four hours a day when you haven't got the time to enjoy the fruits of your labours?'

'Spare me the philosophizing.' Gabriel shifted uncomfortably and shot her a veiled, brooding look because he had heard that refrain a thousand times from his mother until she had eventually given up.

'So what's the point in getting married if you're never going to be around for Luke anyway?'

'Look, shall we go and discuss this somewhere a little more comfortable? These chairs aren't meant for a guy as big as me.'

Which had the immediate effect of distracting Alex in mid-flow as her gaze travelled over him, taking in his drop dead good looks and the spread of his muscular thighs on the small chair.

When she raised her flustered eyes to him, he was grinning at her. 'So,' he drawled, 'where does the good sex feature in this business deal you've agreed to?'

'I…I know what you're trying to do…' Alex licked her lips nervously and wondered at the speed with which she had been derailed.

'What's that?'

'You're trying to distract me.'

'By telling you that I'm not very comfortable in this Goldilocks chair?' To emphasise his point, he shifted and then stood up to flex his muscles. He had rolled up the sleeves of his white work shirt and Alex stared weakly and compulsively at the dark hair on his forearms.

'I was saying…'

'I heard you. You think I'll stick a wedding band on your finger and then disappear back off to work, only to resurface when my son's due to graduate from university.' He took the two steps needed to get to where she was sitting with an expression of rigid intent that Gabriel found strangely cute and endearing, and he bent over to support himself on the arms of her chair.

'You underestimate your pulling power, my darling,' he murmured, stroking her with his voice until her face was red-hot.

'What…what do you mean?'

'You know exactly what I mean. You just want to hear me say it. Shall I tell you, my darling, so that you're in no doubt? Or I could just…' he lowered himself so that he was kneeling in front of her '…show you…hmm…? Do you like me like this…? On my knees in front of you…?'

Alex bit down on the whimper that threatened to escape and tried to give him a stern look, but he was already insinuating himself between her legs and playing with the soft cotton of her T-shirt. When his fingers brushed against the bare skin of her breast, she gasped and half closed her eyes.

'You remembered…' He shoved up the T-shirt and felt the swift kick of hungry craving.

'Remembered what…?'

'How much I like it when you don't wear a bra. I love your breasts. Have I told you that before? But I think I might have forgotten what they taste like…'

'Gabriel!' Alex said in a desperate voice. 'I'm trying to *talk*…'

'And I'm listening. Really. I'm all ears. Don't mind me.'
He delicately tickled the erect bud of her nipple with the tip
of his tongue and when she squirmed and moaned softly, he
had to struggle to contain himself.

'The door…'

'I'll close it.' He quietly shut the kitchen door and then
stood for a few seconds, just looking at her sprawled in the
chair, with her rucked T-shirt and the glistening disc of her
nipple where he had been licking it. Her eyes were half closed
and she was breathing softly.

Talk or no talk, she had agreed to be his wife and he sa-
voured the taste of sweet elation as he strolled lazily to continue what he had started.

CHAPTER NINE

'WE STILL need to talk.' Alex felt that she had let the side down by falling at the first hurdle and making love with him. How could she have the serious talk she had intended on having when his legs were wrapped around hers and the covers were half off their bodies and she could only vaguely remember making her way up the stairs with him to her bedroom?

One minute she was busily trying to get a grip on the situation and the very next minute she had sabotaged her own good intentions and fallen back into bed with him when he'd crooked his finger and given her that smile of his that could unravel every thought in her head. The devastating effect he had had on her senses the first time round was nothing compared to the effect he was capable of having on her now. She closed her eyes in resigned despair as he pushed back her hair and deposited a kiss on her forehead.

'So we do. You can't accuse me of not being willing to listen.'

'How could I have a conversation when you were... were...?'

'Having fun with you?' Gabriel laughed throatily, his good humour fully restored after an hour and a half of very satisfying lovemaking. He slipped his hand under the bed cover and idly toyed with her breast, liking the way it responded to his teasing fingers, even though they were both too spent at the moment to take that teasing touch any further.

'There are a few conditions to my marrying you, Gabriel.' Somehow it didn't feel right to be having this kind of conversation when she was lying naked next to him, nor did she want to spoil the atmosphere of contentment between them but she knew the sort of man he was, the sort who would take her acquiescence for granted and expect her to do as she was told the minute that wedding ring was on her finger. Right now, she had a certain power over him because he fancied her but that power had a time limit and it was important for her to speak her mind now. Or forever, she thought with ironic humour, hold her peace.

'*Conditions?* What are you talking about? What kind of *conditions*?' He propped himself up on his elbow and looked at her with a perplexed frown.

'I don't want to live in London. I gave it a try because I felt that I had to escape and do something for myself after I had Luke and was back on my feet, but I prefer living in the country. I'm not saying that I want to move back to Ireland or anything like that, but I'd like to have some greenery around. Maybe somewhere just outside London so that it wouldn't be too much of a headache for you to commute in.'

'Agreed.'

'You agree? Just like that?'

'Do you think it might be more fun if I argued? Granted, make up sex can be good but it's not worth the effort in this instance.' Gabriel lay back, hands folded behind his head and stared up at the ceiling. Being the dispenser of someone else's wishes felt good and, whilst he had never, not even for a passing second, considered living anywhere but in the thick of it, the prospect of a slightly less frenetic pace of life was not necessarily a bad thing. Train links into central London were quick and Luke would benefit from country living. What kid wouldn't? Fresh air, open spaces…all that corny stuff countryphiles were ever eager to mouth on about now seemed a good idea.

'What sort of house did you have in mind? Country manor? Thatched cottage? No, maybe not that. Converted chapel? Georgian splendour? Give me some details and I can get my people working on it.'

Alex was torn between amusement and annoyance. In Gabriel's world, where having exactly what you wanted was only the snap of a finger away, choosing a house would really not even constitute a minor inconvenience. People to source the right one in the right place, whatever the cost and just maybe one viewing so that the box could be ticked and the green light given.

'Which brings me to my next condition,' Alex said carefully, which earned her another frowning glance.

'What is this?' Gabriel asked, controlling his irritation with difficulty. 'A lesson for me on how to jump through hoops? I should tell you that that particular form of exercise isn't something I plan on getting used to.'

'Marriage is about compromise. I happen to be compromising a lot to marry you because I think it would be right for Luke.' That sounded a great deal more noble than it felt because she couldn't think of a single thing she wouldn't toss to the four winds for the man lying next to her. 'And I want him to be brought up with the values I grew up with,' she continued hurriedly. 'Respect for other people and determination to work hard. I don't want him thinking that he's better than anyone else because his father happens to have a bit of money.'

'I have more than a bit.'

'Having a house appear out of nowhere, like magic, isn't the right way for him to start learning those life lessons.'

'You are the most difficult woman in the world to please! You want to move to the country. I agree. But that's not enough.' He leapt out of bed and Alex sat up in consternation.

'Where are you going?'

'To take a shower.'

'But I'm talking to you!'

'You're not talking to me!' Gabriel headed towards the connecting door to her en suite bathroom, the single most important luxury Alex had looked for when she had bought the house. 'You're laying down rules and regulations.'

'That's what people do with business arrangements!'

'Since when does sex enter a business arrangement?' Gabriel threw over his shoulder and she glared at him because, even when she was mad at him, she still found him so sinfully sexy that she could barely take her eyes off him.

'It's called fringe benefits.'

Gabriel would have slammed the bathroom door behind him but Luke would probably come flying into the bedroom from the sound of it reverberating through the tiny house and there was no way that he wanted his son to see him in this mood. *Business arrangement! Fringe benefits!* He found both descriptions outrageously offensive, even though he was pretty sure he had used those terms himself in the past.

'That's not the language I expect any woman of mine to use,' he informed her coldly, before shutting the bathroom door behind him.

It took a few seconds before Alex was galvanised into action and she scrambled off the bed, hastily flinging on underwear, her T-shirt and a pair of stretchy drawstring shorts from a drawer before pushing open the bathroom door and being greeted by a wall of condensation.

'I'm sorry you don't like the language I use—' her voice was trembling and her knuckles were white as she gripped the sides of the toilet seat, which was the only place to sit in the small bathroom '—but I'm trying really hard to get a perspective on this.' Did he think that, because she fell into his arms, her principles would also obey the same laws and collapse without putting up a fight? 'I don't want something as big as a house purchase to be without our involvement. Luke should have a say in the kind of home we're going to provide for him and so should I. Money might be a convenience but time is priceless and that's what I want you to put into this marriage. I know it's going to be difficult for you because you're accustomed to doing exactly what you want but...' Her voice was suddenly very loud as the shower was switched off and Gabriel stepped out of the cubicle, which he dwarfed.

He took his time drying and then slung the towel around his waist. 'I have taken more time off in the past few weeks than I ever have in my whole life.' Except when he had first met her. He had behaved out of character then as well. 'And, if it means so much to you, then we can look for a house together.'

Alex smiled with relief and followed him out of the room. 'That's great. So...'

'So...?' Having brought no clothes with him, he contented himself with a baggy old bathrobe of hers which was hanging on a hook behind the door, then he took a seat at her dressing table and folded his arms. If getting her on board meant listening to everything she had to say, then so be it, but he didn't intend to be a pushover.

'There's just one more thing.'

'Just the *one more*? I'm shocked. I thought we were here for the rest of the night with your list of provisos and conditions.'

Alex flushed. 'It concerns other women.'

'*Other women?*' Gabriel couldn't believe what he was hearing. He realised that the thought of another woman hadn't actually crossed his mind since he had met Alex again after all this time.

'Yes. Other women. You have to promise me that there won't be any.'

'What kind of a promise is that?' Gabriel threw his hands up in the air in a gesture of frustration. He had had a lifetime of doing exactly what he wanted when it came to the opposite sex. He had power, money, good looks and status and that had all been enough to ensure compliance in the female sex. Even Cristobel had recognised his boundaries and had steered clear of them. He felt his hackles rise at the thought of someone dictating what he could or couldn't do. The question of whether he wanted to or not didn't come into it.

What sort of loser tolerated a woman dictating his every movement? Certainly not him!

'I think if we're to take this whole thing seriously, then…'

'This is getting more ridiculous by the minute. Who knows what's going to happen in the future? Do you think I have a crystal ball stashed away somewhere?'

Alex shook her head mutely. It had been a stupid request but his refusal to give it house room was telling. This wasn't a guy who loved her and would be overjoyed to forswear all other women. Duty to his son might run bone-deep but he had no responsibilities to *her*.

Could she marry someone who would be a hero, but only when on show?

She thought back to Cristobel, to her smug, sly, knowing smile when she had explained to Alex that Gabriel was a Spaniard, that sooner or later he would find his eyes straying, that that was to be expected.

She thought back to what he had told her, that if she didn't marry him then he would inevitably take his attentions elsewhere. She remembered all too well the sick, cloying feeling that had generated in her. Right now, Gabriel wanted her physically. It was a bonus to a marriage which, in his eyes, was the inevitable consequence of their situation.

But Gabriel was a man accustomed to variety. He lived life in the fast lane and the past few weeks spent with her and his son were probably the most normal he had ever had. He had made a huge effort to spend time with them, had set aside his compulsion to work and had condensed his essential business conversations to those times when she was either asleep or else involved with Luke. It would have constituted a big sacrifice and yet, here she was, like an unwelcome drill sergeant, dishing out orders and expecting obedience.

In her desperation to build up her defences and set some rules that might erect walls around her vulnerable core, she had overlooked one very important thing. Gabriel didn't take orders and certainly not from a woman to whom he had no bone-deep emotional connection. They were bound together by Luke but a child could only provide so much glue to a relationship.

And didn't she want this marriage to work? Wasn't that why she had raced back to London so that she could accept his proposal?

From her muddled train of thought there slowly emerged the clarity of her options. She could either love Gabriel in silence and wait hopelessly for the day when he got bored of her or she could do her damnedest to *make* him love her. She could be a passive victim or she could fight for her man.

Yes, it was galling to think that all those sweet dreams of a guy who would fly to the moon and back for her were no longer on the cards, but whoever said that love was a walk in the park? She had loved Gabriel years ago and it had got her nowhere and here she was again, loving him even more, and, unless she did her own groundwork, it would get her nowhere in the end again.

She drew in a deep shaky breath and eventually gave him a rueful, conciliatory smile.

'You're right. It was crazy of me to ask the impossible of you.'

'Are you saying that you don't think me capable of fidelity?' Gabriel growled aggressively and Alex bit back the temptation to tell him what a *difficult* man he could be. His personality was one of extremes. It was why she loved him. He made her feel alive.

'I wish you wouldn't put words in my mouth, Gabriel. I never said that.'

Gabriel ignored that interruption. 'No. But you imply that I am the sort of man who would marry a woman and then proceed to bring a harem of mistresses into the marital home. In front of my son!'

'You look really silly in that bathrobe,' Alex said, to defuse the tension.

'You're trying to change the subject.'

'I'm trying to tell you that it was a stupid condition and I shouldn't have said anything.'

Never one to dwell on imaginary scenarios, Gabriel's mind did a swift detour and began to rocket down an altogether different road. 'Is this whole fidelity issue your way of looking for some kind of excuse to have outside relationships?'

'What?'

'You heard me. I'm not going to repeat myself.'

'Of course that wasn't what I was implying! I'm not that devious!' Alex tried and failed to get her head round the concept of having another guy share her bed. 'But if I *did*,' she couldn't resist adding, 'would you be jealous?'

It was one of those rare instances when Gabriel felt put on the spot and he instinctively shied away from committing himself to any kind of answer.

'I am not a jealous man. I never have been.'

But you would be if you loved me, Alex thought sadly, pinning a brave smile to her face.

'Okay.'

'Which isn't to say that I'm not possessive.' He thought it better to clear up that little issue, once and for all. 'If I thought that you had even looked at another guy when you were wearing my ring on your finger, I would beat him to a pulp.' A red mist descended on him when he thought of her with someone else and he expertly fielded that uncomfortable thought by shoving it to the back of his mind.

That was something, she thought, with a definite lift of her spirits.

'I'm glad we cleared the air,' she confessed, walking towards him. She reached out and clasped her hands behind his neck. 'It's good to talk.'

Gabriel grunted and she perched on his lap and slipped her hand under the fold of the bathrobe.

'You should keep some clothes here.'

'Why? You won't be here much longer.' The feel of her fingers splayed on his chest was doing decidedly pleasant things to other parts of his body.

On this front, at least, Alex was assured of her power over him, temporary though it might be. Just so long as he desired her, he would not have eyes for anyone else. Gabriel, if nothing else, was a one woman man.

'True,' she conceded. 'I'll break the news to my folks tomorrow.'

'And we can make this legal by the end of next week.'

'Why so soon?'

Good question, Gabriel thought. She wasn't the blushing bride with his baby inside her, rushing down the aisle to seal the deal before the baby was born.

'Why not?' he answered smoothly. 'I'm not someone who enjoys delay once I'm committed in a certain direction. Besides, the faster you leave this dump, the better for all concerned.'

'We could just move in with you and take it slowly until we find our feet.'

'No can do.' Gabriel was a little disconcerted at just how much he really *didn't* want that outcome.

'Oh. Forgot. Demands of tradition.'

'That's right. *Demands of tradition.* Not that you won't be moving in with me as soon as possible. In fact, I can arrange for everything to be completed by tomorrow evening.'

'There you go. Not consulting me again.'

'Do you ever agree to anything without putting up a fight?' He shifted her, settling her comfortably on his hard body, letting her know how much he wanted her.

'Would you prefer me to be grateful and submissive?'

'Is that a serious question?'

Alex realised that it was and she was strangely relieved when he said, with an amused smile, 'If you were grateful and submissive, I wouldn't know what had hit me. I would have to take you to a doctor to get you checked over.'

'I find gratitude and submission hard to do,' she conceded truthfully. 'I bet Cristobel was grateful and submissive.' She could have kicked herself for bringing that contentious subject to the table.

'She was...obedient. I've since discovered that obedience is not all that it's made out to be when it comes to women. Not enough of a challenge.'

Alex was busily wondering whether being described as *challenging* was a good thing or a bad thing when Gabriel interrupted her furious musings.

'And, while we're on the subject of rules and conditions, I have a few of my own…'

'Am I going to like them?' she asked cautiously. She gasped as his hand found her breast and he played with it, rolling his finger over her erect nipple and sending shivers of excitement through her.

'First of all, you're going to have to dress the part of my wife.'

'You can't be serious.'

'Deadly serious.'

Alex envisaged smart designer wear and diamonds the size of eggs on her fingers and shuddered. She had seen Cristobel in action. An advert for everything money could possibly buy. The woman had dripped jewellery and screamed *designer*. Every inch of her had been polished, buffed and preened to expensive perfection.

'I can't.'

'What's that supposed to mean? Can I remind you of the compromise conversation you insisted on having earlier?'

'I can't turn into a decorative Christmas bauble for your benefit, Gabriel.'

'What the hell are you talking about?'

'Bejewelled up to the eyeballs…long red talons for nails… big coiffured hair, lacquered to within an inch of its miserable life…'

Gabriel threw back his head and laughed and he laughed even harder when he saw her frowning, disdainful expression. Of one thing he was in no doubt—Alex was not impressed by his vast wealth. In fact, he would have wagered his soul that if she had met him all those years ago and had known the vast legacy that was his birthright, she would have turned on her rubber-soled trainers and stomped off.

'I haven't got sufficient imagination to picture you… What was it…? *Bejewelled up to the eyeballs*…? With long red nails and big hair…?'

'I've seen your ex-fiancée in action,' Alex retorted tartly. 'And I'm not going blonde either. I never held with the myth that they have more fun.'

'I'd never ask you to go blonde. And, before you launch into another wild interpretation of what I want, all I'm saying is that when you're my wife…no, let's just say from the second you set foot out of the house tomorrow…no revealing clothes. No tight dresses, no handkerchiefs for skirts…' He wasn't sure when it had hit him that he didn't want other men ogling her, but hit him it had and, since she felt free and easy to lay down her laws, then two could play at that game.

'I don't own any tight dresses.'

'Good! Then no change there would work for me.'

'I can't remember Cristobel dressing like a frump.' Alex frowned, bewildered by this proviso. 'In fact, when I went shopping with her that time, I seem to recall that she was dressed in a very, very revealing outfit. Right down to the killer heels.'

'Not sure where you're going with this…'

'How come there's one rule for her and another rule for me?'

'Like I said…I'm possessive when it comes to you. Learn to live with it.'

Never having had a devious bone in her body, Alex blushed as she entered a large tick in the column in her head that was dedicated to winning Gabriel over. He might not love her in the same way that she loved him, but possessiveness was a far cry from indifference. Plus, he hadn't been possessive when it came to Cristobel. That had to say something.

'Okay,' she said airily. 'I'm not into all that girlie dressing for men stuff, anyway…'

'Oh, I wouldn't take it too far,' Gabriel murmured. 'You can dress in anything you want, but for my eyes only. Or,' he continued, shoving up her top and losing himself in the sight of her fabulous breasts, 'you can dress in nothing at all.' He could no longer resist and an arrow of pure burning white heat shot through her as he took one nipple into his mouth and proceeded to suckle it with lazy, concentrated intensity. As if suckling that nipple was the only thing in the world he wanted to do at that precise moment in time.

Except it wasn't, as he laid down his number two condition. Which was her duty as his wife to make sure that he was satisfied at all times.

With any other man, this would have been a breathtakingly chauvinistic statement and one which would have had Alex's hackles rising but she was ashamed of the flood of warmth that invaded her body at his boldly assertive declaration.

It might seem crude to wage war on a man's defences through sex but Gabriel was a highly sexual man and the longer she kept him entertained in that department, the more time she had to win him over in the department that really mattered. And entertaining him in that department, she sheepishly acknowledged to herself, was never going to be a sacrifice, was it? One touch from him and she melted like tinder in an inferno.

She would learn how to cook as well. Wasn't that other route to a man's heart through his stomach? They did an awful lot of eating out and she couldn't picture Gabriel as the sort of man who had ever spent time encouraging his women to read recipe books so that they could whip him up some paella like his mother used to make. The opposite, in fact. But, as his wife, surely that wouldn't be a bad idea? Surely domesticity could creep up on him and stage an invasion before he knew what was happening to him?

If nothing worked, if lust turned out to be a passing pleasure and Luke was really and truly the only reason he would stay with her, then he would eventually stray but she didn't want to think about that. She made love with the passion of sheer optimism and, afterwards, enjoyed the contentment of just lying in his arms and hearing the soft beating of his heart.

'What are your thoughts on home-cooked food?' she asked dreamily.

'I can't say I have any,' Gabriel replied with lazy amusement.

'Why do you think that is?' She shifted on to one elbow and tried very hard not to look at him with puppy dog eyes. The irony of knowing just how thorough her U-turn had been didn't escape her. Not only had she descended from her un-assailable position of wanting to stand firm and maintain a healthy distance from the guy who had lied to her and sub-sequently dumped her, she had positively burnt the map so that she could never, ever find her way back to that safe place again.

'Why cook meals when someone else can cook them better in a restaurant? I know where this is going,' he added dryly, and Alex feigned bewilderment. 'Don't worry. You don't want Luke to have a precious upbringing. I get it. I agree with you. I'll hire a cook. No problem.'

Alex smiled, unwilling to become embroiled in a circuitous argument about what constituted a *precious upbringing* and what didn't. She was amused that Gabriel's solution to the dilemma of eating out wasn't a loyalty card to a supermarket but hiring a chef. He inhabited a different world to the one she knew but, bit by bit, she would make inroads into his world and change him.

His mobile gave its sharp intrusive buzz and he picked up the call, turning away from her and speaking in rapid Spanish. Business. She half listened to the conversation, bored by talk of share options and cost projections. She let her mind wander pleasantly and tried not to run her hands along his back in a nauseatingly loving manner. Thinking of herself as controlling the situation did her no end of good but she was still bitterly disappointed when he ended his call and turned to her with a regretful expression.

'Crisis at work, *cara*. I know you'd rather I was around twenty-four seven but…' he shrugged and smiled ruefully '…I'm going to have to fly to New York for a few days. Might even be as long as a week.'

Alex laughed and raked her fingers through her short dark hair, ruffling it so that it stood up in boyish spikes.

'What makes you think that I want you around twenty-four seven?'

Gabriel frowned. 'Your little speech about wanting me to spend time with you?'

'Time with *Luke*.' She beamed at him. However rosy her plans were for capturing him, she still didn't intend for him to think that she was on her hands and knees begging for scraps of his attention. 'So you can put that gigantic ego of yours away. Actually, I'm perfectly happy in your absence. I can start doing a little packing, just books and ornaments and stuff. I won't look for a job yet if we might be moving further out of London. Hmm. Maybe,' she mused aloud, 'I'll go visit my family in Ireland. Mum's been complaining that she misses Luke and I can tell them about the wedding plans first-hand.'

Gabriel was disconcerted to feel a twinge of annoyance at this sudden, cheerfully independent plan of action. Of course it made perfect sense for her to talk to her family face to face! She was very close to them.

'You'll have to give me your landline there.' He squashed the ridiculous notion that he wanted her to be there at his beck and call and certainly not grinning when he told her that he was going to be out of the country.

'Why? I'll take my mobile.'

'No can do. You're not good at remembering to charge it. What if I need to get in touch with you?'

Alex shrugged and rattled off her parents' telephone number although, at the end of it, went on to say that she might change her mind.

'Woman's prerogative. I might just get Mum and Dad to come down to London. They haven't been in ages. So I'm not sure. I'll let you know.' Another broad smile.

Gabriel grunted. His timescale for the wedding was short-ening by the second. He didn't like this house. He didn't like the fact that he had to trek halfway across London to see his son, particularly as he had become accustomed to having him around. And he didn't like Alex thinking that she could skip around wherever and whenever she wanted like a single girl. Which she wasn't. Who knew if there was some guy lurking back in her home town? Naturally, he wasn't going to express any concern in that area but, if she was married, there would be none of this nonsense. He decided that he would cut short his trip to New York by a day or two. There was no need for him to sit in on every single meeting and hold Edwards's hand. Time the man stepped up to the mark.

Alex surreptitiously looked at him, proud that she had put on such a good show of not looking deflated at the thought

er to make a great big deal of it. Just
something hot and homely and heartwarming.

And she really would have, but something was slipped
under her door two days later that would blow all her plans
to smithereens…

CHAPTER TEN

THE neatly clipped newspaper page was accompanied by a saccharine note that read: *I thought you should see this*. Alex had just dropped Luke off to his playgroup and done some shopping; the envelope lying on the mat inside the door must have been hand-delivered. She stared at the picture for ages, during which time life seemed to slow to a standstill.

Gabriel was, as always, distinctive, his proud, arrogant head inclined down towards Cristobel's uplifted face. Had Cristobel delivered the clipping? Of course she had! Who else? It was from an American tabloid. What had she been doing in New York? Suddenly a host of sickening doubts and misgivings rushed through Alex like a swarm of locusts, devouring everything in its path. She dumped the shopping bags on the floor and sat down so that she could give the picture one hundred per cent of her attention.

Gabriel had spoken to her on the telephone twice since he had left the country and she had spent ages talking to him, chatting about nothing in particular, content to enjoy the rich, lazy drawl of his voice and to hear about what he had been doing. Now she wondered whether Cristobel had been in the hotel room whilst he had made those calls. Maybe she had been tapping her long scarlet nails and looking at her diamond watch as she had impatiently waited for him to wrap it up.

In complete turmoil, Alex found that she couldn't concentrate at all for the remainder of the day. She had intended to start packing away some of her possessions, boxing up the ones she would take with her to her new house. Her new life! Now, it all seemed pointless. She would have fought tooth and nail to turn her charade of a marriage into something meaningful, but seeing that picture of Cristobel with Gabriel had shown her that there was nothing to fight over and to carry on kidding herself otherwise would have reduced her to the level of a joke.

She wondered if she should just pack her bags and return to Ireland. Should she? What would be the point of that? Gabriel would find her and he wouldn't be pleased.

It was all too easy to project a scenario in which Gabriel hunted her down and used his mighty power and influence to take Luke away from her. Would he do that? Previously she would have sworn with one hand on the Bible that he would never have been capable of any such thing, but just how well did she know him? Hadn't her very first meeting with him been based on a lie? Hadn't he manipulated a situation years ago because it had suited him at the time? He had pretended to be someone he wasn't and he had told her that it was because anonymity had given him a taste of freedom for a while but couldn't it equally have been true that he had sussed her within seconds and realised that she wasn't the kind of girl who found rich, spoiled men attractive? And so he had cleverly *dropped the trappings and adopted a different cover?*

Alex hated thinking like that, but she couldn't deny the grainy photo of Gabriel and Cristobel together. The bags of shopping, lots of food items in preparation for the Domestic Goddess she was to become, lay on the floor cruelly mocking her fanciful, pie-in-the-sky dreams.

By seven that evening she was ready for bed and was so spent from her troubled thoughts that she failed to stir when the phone rang at ten. And rang. And rang.

Frustrated, Gabriel raked his fingers through his hair and stared at his mobile. No reply from the landline and her cellphone was switched off. He had never met a woman who was so disorganised when it came to her mobile phone. It was seldom charged and, when it was, it was continually programmed on silent so that phone calls were routinely missed because she couldn't hear it ring and, when she did hear it, locating the thing in her oversized bag was an accomplishment based solely on luck.

He would have to phone her in the morning. He would never have credited it, but whereas women had always run a poor second to work, Alex seemed to fly in the face of this immutable truth. He thought about her way too much when she wasn't around and especially now, when Cristobel had appeared on the scene because she *just happened to be doing some shopping in New York and had heard that he was around from his secretary*. Out of a misplaced sense of good manners and residual guilt, he had taken her to dinner and had had a first hand opportunity to see for himself just how inconsequential Cristobel had been to him. It astounded him that he had ever found himself drifting into an engagement to her. For someone who prided himself on his astute judgement and razor-sharp acumen, he realised that he had very nearly sleep-walked himself into the worst situation of his life.

He had been struck by a strong sense of gratitude that he now had Alex and Luke in his life. Frankly, he found it difficult to remember a time when he didn't, which was weirdly comforting and confusing at the same time.

When, the following day, he tried calling again, this time at six in the morning, when she surely could be nowhere else but in the house, and received no answer, a sense of foreboding edged its way past his initial concern.

He had a series of meetings lined up and he did his best to concentrate on the business of sealing this deal, but his thoughts were elsewhere.

Had she decided to go and visit her parents in Ireland? On the spur of the moment, he dialled the landline number she had given him and the phone was answered by a woman who confirmed that her parents were away and wouldn't be back for another week. He had to cut short a rambling description of where they had gone and how long overdue the holiday had been.

Never again would Gabriel underestimate the power of his imagination. Unable to get through to her, he could only think that a disaster had occurred. His palms grew clammy and he began to feel sick as he thought of various scenarios involving hospitals and emergency rooms. Had Luke been taken ill? Surely Alex would have called him immediately if that had been the case? The answer to that was yes. With lightning speed, his thoughts veered off that train of thought to a more likely one: Alex had had an accident of some sort and had been unable to get through to him.

Once planted in his head, he was unable to shake the feeling that something was disastrously wrong.

Gabriel was not of the temperament to sit around twiddling his thumbs and stressing and he was honest enough to admit that no amount of high level meetings had the power to distract. He was a man of action and, in a move that would have shocked anyone who knew him well, he delegated the remainder of what needed doing to the members of the board who had accompanied him on the trip to New York. He had always been pivotal in any talks of strategic importance but he had to concede that if the deal fell through, then the deal fell through. No amount of success in this matter was worth the way his mind was going off the rails.

Not for the first time, he missed the availability of *Concorde* for transatlantic speed. However, his name carried sufficient weight to ensure that he was sitting in the next available first class cabin leaving New York.

He would have had a very hard time admitting it to anyone, but he felt out of control and he breathed a sigh of relief when the plane finally landed at Heathrow.

In possession of hand luggage only, he was out of the airport in record time and heading for her house without bothering to detour past his apartment.

Three loud bangs on the door had Alex almost spilling the cup of coffee she had made, her first for the day. In an effort to conceal her terrible frame of mind, she had spent the past day and a half over-compensating with Luke and had had a hellish time trying to settle him in bed after two bowls of ice cream and a chocolate bar. She knew that Gabriel had been trying to get hold of her and she had taken care to ignore his persistent ringing because she just didn't trust herself not to lash out at him. He had also tried her mobile. She had seen the missed calls and had erased them, furious with herself for having got herself all tangled up again, just like she had before, hopelessly loving a guy who was so bad for her.

Her whole body tensed with shock as she pulled open the door to find Gabriel standing in front of her, the lines of his strong face tense.

'Gabriel! What are you doing here? You're not due back for a couple of days…' Her voice trailed off as he strode past her into the small hallway, turning at the bottom of the stairs to look at her with a dark, shuttered expression.

Alex quietly shut the door and leaned against it. She hadn't had time to brace herself to face him. Now, she was all over the place. Her heart was hammering inside her and she had broken out in a fine film of nervous perspiration. Why had he returned early? Surely it had something to do with Cristobel. The coincidence was just too uncanny otherwise.

'I've been trying to get through to you,' Gabriel said tightly. He stared at her across the width of the hall, his keen dark eyes taking in her nerves and wondering what the hell was going on.

'Yes, I know.'

'You knew but you chose not to take my calls?'

'Have you come straight from the airport? Why?'

Relief that she was all right, as was Luke, or she would have said something, mingled now with anger and a certain amount of confusion.

'I…was worried about you both,' Gabriel said heavily. 'Can you blame me? I was thousands of miles away, with no idea what was going on over here.'

'Sorry,' Alex mumbled, looking down at her silly bedroom slippers. Even with her mind doing crazy loops in her head and her heart splintering into a thousand pieces, she was still aware of the fact that she would have changed into something a little more attractive had she known that he was going to descend on her. Instead, she was wearing her oldest track pants and a T-shirt with a comical motif that had faded to the point of obscurity after a million washes.

'So?' he prompted harshly, because she appeared to have frozen into immobility. 'Care to tell me what's going on? I dropped everything to get over here.'

Alex thought of him abandoning his meetings and his conferences so that he could fly back to London and fought against that desperate treacherous tendency to read something significant into his behaviour.

'Maybe we should go into the sitting room,' she mumbled, edging away from the front door with her arms firmly folded in front of her.

'Not until you tell me what's going on. I worked out it couldn't be Luke or you would have picked up my calls. Which led me to think that something might have happened to you.'

'Something like what?'

'Oh, for God's sake! What do you think? Some kind of… of accident…'

'And don't pretend you would have cared one jot!' Alex blurted out, tears springing to her eyes so that she had to stare back down at the ground again and gather herself.

The silence bristled between them. Gabriel had the strangest *now or never* feeling. What was he supposed to do with that?

'There's something you need to see,' Alex continued in a shaky, driven voice and she walked quickly past him, towards the sitting room and her handbag, where that wretched newspaper clipping had taken up residence in her wallet and had been steadily burning a hole in it for the past few interminable days.

Gabriel watched, mystified and irrationally panic stricken as she rummaged in her oversized sack and finally withdrew a piece of paper which she handed silently over to him.

It took him a few seconds to recognise Cristobel, staring up at him for all the world as though they were lovers. He hadn't even been aware of any paparazzi around at the time. He could just remember feeling impatient and keen to see the back of her. Unfortunately, that had not been transmitted in the shot, artfully snapped to fabricate a story out of nothing.

'She came to see me after you had left the island. I didn't tell you. She said that she would have you back, but I didn't want to believe her…'

Gabriel tore his eyes away from the newspaper clipping and then he quietly scrunched it between his fingers and tossed it on to the table between them. He shoved his hands in his pockets and reluctantly raised his eyes to hers.

'You wanted me to marry you because of Luke and the second I accepted, you resumed your…your…' Her head ached with the effort of not crying but her voice was unsteady and, since she couldn't look at him, she looked instead at the crumpled piece of evidence on the table. 'Would you ever have told me that you'd met Cristobel in New York if she hadn't been kind enough to provide proof of it?'

'There was nothing to tell.'

'Nothing to *you*, maybe.'

'I'm not…in the habit of explaining my actions to anyone. Well…I never was…'

'I can't be married to a man who doesn't think that he's accountable at all to his wife. I know that appearances for you are everything, but how do you think it makes me feel to realise that you're happy to take up where you left off with your ex-fiancée? Cristobel would have no problem sneaking around with you behind my back. Apparently that's *the Spanish way*. Whatever *that's* supposed to mean. I guess she just meant that that's *your way*. Marry because you have an overdeveloped sense of obligation but then just carry on doing exactly what you want!'

'She must have set the whole thing up…'

'Is that *all* you have to say, Gabriel? That *she must have set the whole thing up?*' Alex clenched her fists tightly and tears of bitter disappointment and frustration pricked the backs of her eyes. The cold, sickening realisation that this would be the soundtrack of her marriage, were she to marry him, swept over her with torrential force. Building crazy fantasies in her head and nursing girlish dreams of getting him to love her were frankly delusional. She would be entering into a contract, one that would see her financially secure for life, but that was it. No more, no less.

'No.'

'No *what*? Why can't you at least be honest with me?'

'Talking about feelings doesn't come easy for me. I've never been one of those touchy-feely kind of guys…'

'Okay.' Alex turned away, defeated, and walked towards the window, away from him.

'No, it's not okay.' Gabriel raked his fingers through his hair and was gripped with sudden indecision. She wasn't looking at him. She was staring through the window at nothing in particular and he couldn't blame her. If Cristobel had sat and plotted for a thousand years, she couldn't have come up with a better way of getting her own back on him for her ruined marriage plans. And how had he reacted when that horrendous picture had been thrust at him? With virtual silence. Was it any wonder that she couldn't bear to set eyes on him?

'I…' he began hesitantly. He shook his head, impatient with himself, and strode towards her, ignoring the way she shied back as she spun around and watched him descending on her.

'I had no idea that Cristobel was going to be in New York,' he said slowly. 'She got me on my mobile, claimed that she just wanted to talk to me, that I owed her that much at least, so I reluctantly agreed to take her out to dinner.'

'Yes, well, I could see reluctance brimming over in that snapshot of the two of you.'

This close to her, he could breathe in her clean soapy scent and the elusive apple and honey fragrance of her recently washed hair.

'Whatever you see in that photo,' he murmured, 'you're way off target. The dinner was only successful in so far as it made me see what a damn fool I had been to have ever became engaged to Cristobel. Not only is she a vain, shallow person, but there was a spitefulness there that repelled me.'

'You're just saying that,' Alex whispered.

'She must have planned the whole thing, right down to making sure that someone would be there to capture us on camera. She knows that there's no hope in hell that I'll ever have anything more to do with her, but a woman scorned is still a woman scorned.'

Alex folded her arms and stared at the right sleeve of his shirt.

'You…you do things to me, Alex…'

'Oh, *really*.'

'Yes, *really*.' He tilted her head so that she could look at him and she jerked back. Her eyes were glazed and damp and he felt his heart constrict. 'You do the same things to me that I do to you.'

'What's that?' Alex flung at him, rubbing her leaking eyes with the back of her hand. 'Turn you on?'

'Make me cry.'

At that, Alex looked up at him. Her mouth was parted, ready for attack, but her brain had seized up. She made a soft choking sound and blinked.

'I was an arrogant sod the first time you met me. Too young to realise that you were the best thing to ever happen in my life. You showed up again and I was still an arrogant sod but it didn't take me long to grow accustomed to you. To have you in my head every minute of the day. I can't focus when you're not around. You complete me.'

Alex's eyes were like saucers. For someone who didn't do the touchy-feely stuff, he seemed pretty spectacular right now and she didn't want the moment to end.

'You're gaping.' He gave her a crooked smile. He risked touching her, just a feathery brush of his finger along her cheek. 'I love you, Alex, and if you still want to walk away from marrying me then I won't try to stop you.'

'You *love* me? Why didn't you ever *say*?'

'I didn't recognise it, my darling. How was I to know that love was something that could ram into you when you weren't looking with the force of a freight train? How was I to spot that the first sign would be when your sense of complete control starts unravelling?'

Alex smiled, then she beamed and then she reached up and stroked his face. 'And I love you too. I never stopped, Gabriel. Even when I was as mad as hell with you, I still loved you. That's why I agreed to marry you. After Cristobel came and spouted all that stuff about you being the sort of Spaniard who would lose interest in me, I knew that I had to do whatever I could to turn what you felt for me into something strong enough to see us through.'

She closed her eyes and reached up, her mouth searching for his, her lips parting as he kissed her with fierce, burning hunger. She whimpered when he eventually pulled back to look down at her with such loving eyes that her heart skipped a beat.

'So you'll marry me…' he murmured huskily.

'You wouldn't be able to stop me.'

'You wait and see,' Gabriel promised solemnly. 'I will be the best father, the best husband, the best lover and the best friend you will ever have.'

A sigh of pure contentment escaped her lips. She curled her arms around his neck and sighed again when his hand cupped her breast with possessive intimacy.

'Right back at you,' she whispered.

EPILOGUE

THOSE missed years could never be replaced but Alex was good at not allowing Gabriel to beat himself up over that. The present was all that mattered and the present was a pretty wonderful place to be, he had to concede.

Luke was now seven and the apple of his father's eye. Indeed, Gabriel could hardly remember that time when he had lived and breathed work. His life had been one-dimensional, he now realised, although if someone had said so to him at the time he wouldn't have had a clue where they were coming from.

'I blame you,' he mused aloud, as Alex slid into the chair opposite him.

They had returned to the island to celebrate their third wedding anniversary, having left Luke with his grandparents in Spain. The housekeepers had been dispatched and here was his beloved wife now, dressed in a floaty cream creation which he would enjoy removing very, very slowly in a couple of hours' time.

Food had been prepared by Ana, who was still their loyal retainer at the house, and Alex was doing the honours. *I may not be a brilliant cook*, she had laughed, *but I'm good at heating things up*.

'Blame me for what?' She grinned because, over time, she was discovering just how complex this man of hers was.

'I've been domesticated.'

Alex sipped her champagne and smiled, leaning across the table and cupping her face in her hand. 'It's inevitable, I'm afraid.'

'So your mother told me the last time we visited them. Your married brothers have become pussycats.'

What he had anticipated as being a difficult relationship had been surprisingly easy. Alex's parents had accepted him without fuss and, although her brothers had initially given him a few filthy looks, they had grudgingly allowed him into their hallowed circle when he had proved himself knowledgeable on most things Irish. After some consolidated help from the Internet on his part. Now he had fun outsmarting them on their own turf, although they had wised up to his tactics and were always polishing up new ways to catch him out.

'Nice dress, by the way,' he murmured, angling his body so that he could nudge his thigh against her leg under the table. 'I'm going to enjoy taking it off. All those little buttons at the front. Could be an interesting challenge.'

Their eyes met and Alex felt that wonderful whoosh in her stomach that always happened when he was with her.

'You have a one track mind,' she teased, laughing.

'And you're always the woman at the end of that track.'

'Quite right!'

'The past three years have been the best of my life,' Gabriel told her seriously. 'I always thought that I was a pretty relaxed kind of guy. I was wrong. You taught me how to kick back. You and Luke…' he cleared his throat, just in case his voice did something stupid like sound unsteady '…you mean everything to me.'

'Which is terrific…' Alex stroked the side of his face with her hand and smiled tenderly at this brilliant man who was her own breath of life '…just so long as there's room in there for a little more love because I'm pregnant.'

Gabriel stood up and tugged her to her feet, his smile warm and loving. His hand moved to curve over her still flat stomach and he thought, with pleasure and with a sense of utter peace and contentment, that this was what it was to be home.

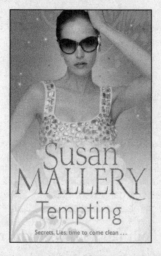
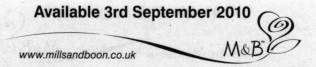

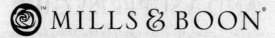

2 FREE BOOKS
AND A SURPRISE GIFT

We would like to take this opportunity to thank you for reading this Mills & Boon® book by offering you the chance to take TWO more specially selected books from the Modern™ series absolutely FREE! We're also making this offer to introduce you to the benefits of the Mills & Boon® Book Club™—

- **FREE home delivery**
- **FREE gifts and competitions**
- **FREE monthly Newsletter**
- **Exclusive Mills & Boon Book Club offers**
- **Books available before they're in the shops**

Accepting these FREE books and gift places you under no obligation to buy, you may cancel at any time, even after receiving your free books. Simply complete your details below and return the entire page to the address below. You don't even need a stamp!

YES Please send me 2 free Modern books and a surprise gift. I understand that unless you hear from me, I will receive 4 superb new books every month for just £3.19 each, postage and packing free. I am under no obligation to purchase any books and may cancel my subscription at any time. The free books and gift will be mine to keep in any case.

Ms/Mrs/Miss/Mr _____ Initials _____

_____

Surname _____

Address _____

_____

_____ Postcode _____

E-mail _____

Send this whole page to: Mills & Boon Book Club, Free Book Offer, FREEPOST NAT 10298, Richmond, TW9 1BR